A GOOD SCHOOL

Also by Richard Yates

A GOOD SCHOOL

a novel by

Richard Yates

Picador
Henry Holt and Company
New York

www.picadorusa.com

Picador® is a U.S. registered trademark and is used by Henry Holt and Company under license from Pan Books Limited.

For information on Picador Reading Group Guides, as well as ordering, please contact the Trade Marketing department at St. Martin's Press.
Phone: 1-800-221-7945 extension 763
Fax: 212-677-7456
E-mail: trademarketing@stmartins.com

Lyrics from "Good Night Sweetheart" by Ray Noble, Jimmy Campbell and Reg Connelly: Copyright © 1931, renewed 1959 by Campbell, Connelly & Co. Ltd., London, England. Rights throughout the United States and Canada controlled by Robbin Music Corporation, New York, N.Y. Used by permission.

Portions of this work first appeared in *The New York Times Book Review* and *Decade* magazine.

ISBN 0-312-42039-0

First published in the United States by Delacorte Press

D 10 9 8 7 6

To the memory of my father

Draw your chair up close
to the edge of the precipice
and I'll tell you a story.

— F. Scott Fitzgerald

A GOOD SCHOOL

Foreword

As a young man, in upstate New York, my father studied to be a concert tenor. He had a fine, disciplined voice that combined great power with great tenderness; hearing him sing remains the best of my early memories.

I think he sang professionally a few times, in places like Syracuse and Binghamton and Utica, but he wasn't able to make a career of it; instead he became a salesman. I imagine he joined the General Electric Company in Schenectady as a delaying action, in order to have a few dollars coming in while he continued to seek concert engagements, but before very long the company swallowed him up. By the time he was forty, when I was born, he had long since come down to

the city and settled into the job he would hold for the rest
of his life, that of an assistant regional sales manager for the
Mazda Lamp Division (light bulbs).

People still asked him to sing at social gatherings —
"Danny Boy" seemed to be the popular favorite among re-
quest numbers — and sometimes he did, but more and more
often in later years he would decline. If pressed, he would
take a backward step and make a little negative wave of the
hand, smiling and frowning at the same time: all that, he
seemed to say — "Danny Boy"; the years upstate; singing
itself — all that was in the past.

His office in the General Electric building was barely big
enough to contain a desk and a framed photograph of my
older sister and myself as small children; it was in that
cubicle that he earned however much money it took to send
my mother what she asked for every month, year after year.
They had been divorced almost as long as I could remember.

He greatly loved my sister — I think that must have been
the main reason for his unflagging generosity to us —
but he and I, after I was eleven or so, seemed always bewil-
dered by each other. There seemed to be an unspoken agreement between us that, in the dividing process of the divorce,
I had been given over to my mother.

There was pain in that assumption — for both of us, I
would guess, though I can't speak for him — yet there was
an uneasy justice in it too. Much as I might wish it otherwise,
I did prefer my mother. I knew she was foolish and irrespon-
sible, that she talked too much, that she made crazy emotional scenes over nothing and could be counted on to collapse in a crisis, but I had come to suspect, dismally, that my
own personality might be built along much the same lines.
In ways that were neither profitable nor especially pleasant,
she and I were a comfort to one another.

The art of sculpture and the idea of aristocracy had always appealed to her equally, and so, after the divorce, she became a sculptor who longed to have rich people admire her work and accept her into their lives. Both her artistic and her social ambitions were forever thwarted, often in humiliating ways, but there were occasional tantalizing moments when everything seemed to be coming together nicely for her.

One of those times occurred in May or June of 1941, when I was fifteen. For the past year or so she had conducted a small weekly sculpture class in her studio, which was also the living room of our Greenwich Village apartment, and one of her students was a rich girl of exceptional beauty and charm named Jane. I think Jane must have romanticized my mother as a struggling artist, as many people seemed to do (I did too); in any case, upon dropping out of the sculpture class to get married, she invited us to attend the wedding.

It was a real Society wedding, held outdoors on Jane's parents' enormous lawn in Westchester County, and we'd never seen anything like it. The groom was almost as stunning as the bride, a young naval officer in a flawless white uniform with a choker collar and stiff black-and-gold epaulets. There was an orchestra, there was a dance floor on a specially-built platform trimmed with white canvas, and there were what seemed hundreds of lovely girls who danced with their partners as soon as Jane and her naval officer had used his fiercely gleaming sword to cut the cake.

I was wearing a cheap, big-shouldered winter suit, badly outgrown, that my father had bought for me at Bond's in Times Square. And if I was uncomfortable, I hate to imagine how my sister must have felt: she was only about a year younger than Jane; she knew none of these splendid boys and girls; her clothes must have been every bit as wrong as mine; and still she trailed along with me after our mother, smiling, moving from one cluster of chattering guests to another over those acres of lawn, nibbling tiny watercress sandwiches.

"Is this boy in school?" a woman's harsh voice inquired.

"Well, actually," my mother said, "I've been trying to think of a school for him, but there are so many schools and it's all so confusing I really — "

"Dorset Academy," the woman said, and now I got a look at her: big, gruff, a good deal of loose flesh under the chin. "It's the only school in the East that understands boys. My boy loved it." She shoved a folded watercress sandwich into her mouth and chewed it mightily. Then, talking around her chewing, she said "Dorset Academy, Dorset, Connecticut. Don't forget it. Write it down. You'll never be sorry."

I wasn't home the day W. Alcott Knoedler, headmaster of Dorset Academy, came to visit my mother in response to her letter of inquiry, but I heard about it afterwards in great detail. The headmaster himself! Wasn't that something? He'd happened to be in New York; he'd had her letter with him; he'd just dropped by to tell her about Dorset. She apologized breathlessly — her studio was a terrible mess; she hadn't been expecting visitors — and when she heard the tuition fee she could only tell him how sorry she was: fourteen hundred dollars was out of the question. And the remarkable thing was that W. Alcott Knoedler didn't go away. Occasionally, he explained, it was possible to arrange a downward adjustment — perhaps even half the normal tuition. Would seven hundred be within her means? Could she consider it, at least? And would she and her son give him the pleasure, later in the summer, of being his guests for a tour of the Dorset campus?

"He was just — I don't know — just the nicest man," she told me. "I can't tell you how nice he was. And it sounds like such an *interesting* school. It's very small, only about a hundred and twenty-five boys, and you see that means each boy gets more personal attention and so on. Oh, and do you know what he said?" Her eyes were bright.

"What?"

"He said 'Dorset believes in individuality.' Doesn't that sound like the perfect kind of school for you?"

Our tour of the campus that July was a delirium of acquiescence. It was, as my mother must have said twenty times, a beautiful place. Dorset Academy lay miles from any town in northern Connecticut. It had been built and founded in the nineteen-twenties by an eccentric lady millionaire named Abigail Church Hooper, often quoted as having said her life's ambition was to establish a school "for the sons of the gentry," and she had spared no expense. All its buildings were of thick, dark red stone in what we were told was "Cotswold" architecture, with gabled slate roofs whose timbers had intentionally been installed when the wood was young so that in aging they would warp and sag in interesting ways. Four long classroom-and-dormitory buildings formed a lovely quadrangle, three stories high and enclosing many big trees. Beyond it, along curving flagstone walks, lay an attractive assortment of other buildings large and small, each with its sagging roofline and its display of deep, expensive lead-casement windows, and there were rich lawns.

But it would take me years to see what brighter people seemed to notice right away, that there was something fanciful and even specious in the very beauty of the place — a prep school that might have been conceived in the studios of Walt Disney. And this was another thing I was a long time in learning, though I suppose I might have guessed it from the tone of the woman's voice at Jane's wedding: Dorset

Academy had a wide reputation for accepting boys who, for any number of reasons, no other school would touch.

Back in New York and filled with high purpose, my mother made an impassioned telephone call to my father, at the office, to get the money. I think it took several such calls, but eventually, as usual, he came through. The academic paperwork was accomplished with surprising dispatch, and I was enrolled as a member of the fourth form (tenth grade), to begin my studies in September.

The next step was to buy my school uniform, for which the men's clothing department at Franklin Simon's held the exclusive franchise. In the daytime, Dorset boys wore tasteful gray tweed suits — the clerk said two of these were customary, but we held the line at one — and there was an option to wear the official Dorset blazer, of burgundy flannel with blue piping and the school crest on its breast pocket, which we declined to buy. There was a separate, mandatory uniform for evening: a double-breasted black jacket and striped trousers, a white shirt with a stiff detachable collar (regular or wing) and a black bow tie.

"Now," my mother said as we left the store. "You're a Dorset boy."

Not quite. The part of the headmaster's spiel that had interested me most was that Dorset boys performed "community service" — they felled trees, they did farm work, they rode around like laborers in the beds of pickup trucks — and so our shopping wasn't complete until I'd taken my mother to an Army and Navy store and picked out the right kind of dungarees and work shirts, the right kind of high-cut work shoes and an imitation Navy pea coat. If all else failed, I felt I could hold my own at Dorset Academy in an outfit like that.

It isn't hard to guess how my father must have felt about

all this. The notion of an expensive boarding school must have struck him as preposterous, and the cost of it must surely have put him into debt. But he was very agreeable about it to me. He took me on a rare visit to his West Side apartment, just the two of us, and served a good dinner of lamb stew that I think his girlfriend must have left simmering on the stove for us that afternoon (I had met her on several nervous occasions, but she'd probably decided to leave us alone that evening). His home was refreshingly clean and neat after the chaotic sculpture shop where I lived; when we'd stacked the dishes we sat around talking for a couple of hours — hesitantly and awkwardly, as always, but I remember thinking we'd done better than usual. And he sent me home that night with two gifts that he thought might be useful for a boy going away to school — a well-worn, heavy suitcase of the old-fashioned kind called a "Boston bag" that finally fell apart during my senior year, and a fitted leather shaving kit, new-looking and stamped with his initials, that stayed with me all through my time in the Army until I lost it somewhere in Germany.

And I imagine he must have been agreeable about it to everyone else. I can picture a scene that might have taken place in the outer office of his floor when he and another employee, in their shirtsleeves, each with a handful of business papers, might have paused to exchange friendly greetings over the all-day clatter of business typewriters. I see the other man as being bigger and heartier than my father, possibly extending his free hand to clasp my father's shoulder.

"How's the family, Mike?" he would say. My father's name was Vincent, but everyone in the office called him "Mike"; I've never known why.

"Oh, they're fine, thanks."

"That pretty little girl of yours gonna be getting married soon?"

"Oh, I don't know — not too soon, I hope; but sure, pretty soon, I suppose."

"You better bet she is. She's a sweetheart. And how's the boy?"

"Well, he'll be going off to prep school in the fall."

"Yeah? Prep school? Jesus, Mike, isn't that costing you an arm and a leg?"

"Well, it's — not cheap, but I think I can handle it."

"Which prep school?"

"Place called Dorset Academy, up in Connecticut."

"Dorset?" the man would say. "Don't think I've ever heard of that one."

And I can see my father starting to turn away then, concluding the pleasantries, looking tired. He wasn't old that summer — he was fifty-five — but within eighteen months he would be dead. "Well," he would say, "as a matter of fact I'd never heard of it either, but it's — you know — it's supposed to be a good school."

Chapter 1

At fifteen, Terry Flynn had the face of an angel and the body of a perfect athlete. He was built on a small scale, but he was utterly beautiful. Walking fully dressed among his friends, he moved with a light, nimble, special grace that set him apart from everyone; just by watching him walk you could picture the way he would leap to catch a forward pass, evade any number of potential tacklers and run alone into the end zone for the winning touchdown as the crowd went wild.

And if Terry looked good in his clothes, that was nothing compared to his performance every day in the dormitory when he stripped, wrapped a towel around his waist and made his way down the hall to the showers. He had what is

called muscle definition: every bulge and cord and ripple of
him was outlined as if by the bite of a classical sculptor's
chisel, and he carried himself accordingly. "Hi, Terry," the
boys would call as he passed, and "Hey, Terry"; within a very
few days after his arrival at Dorset Academy, Terry Flynn
had become the only new boy in Three building to be univer-
sally called by his first name.

In the shower room, which also contained the two toilet
stalls and four sinks on that end of the hall, he was splendid.
He would make a modest little show of whisking the towel
away from his loins, proving he was hung like a horse; then
he would step into the hot spray and stand there posing,
shifting his weight from one foot to the other, a soaked and
glistening statue. The little-finger of his right hand had been
broken once in a football game and never mended properly;
it wouldn't bend, and the delicate stiffness of that finger,
which looked at first like an affectation, lent just the right
note of insouciance to his personality.

Dorset was Terry's fourth prep school, but he was only in
the second form — he was still learning to read — and so his
classmates were not his contemporaries. In the hours before
lunch he associated with his classmates, a cluster of thir-
teen-year-olds each of whom would feel warm and silly all
over whenever Terry smiled at him; the rest of his time he
gave to his contemporaries. His room was the most popular
gathering-place in that section of Three building and was
sometimes honored by the presence of older boys, sixteen-
and seventeen-year-olds, who would drop in to join the horsing around. Terry didn't talk much, but he usually managed
to say the right thing when he did. And he had a memorable
laugh, an explosive "Bubba-*hah!*" that could be heard all up
and down the hall.

"Hey, d'ja hear about Mr. Draper and his home brew?"

someone said on one of these social occasions. Mr. Draper was the chemistry master, a frail man so crippled by polio in all four limbs that he could barely walk and barely hold a pencil. "MacKenzie had to go over to the lab last night to get a book or some damn thing, and when he turned on the lights there's Draper on the floor, flat on his back, waving his arms and legs around in the air like some — you know, like some bug tryna turn himself over? So MacKenzie gets down and picks him up — he says he only weighs about sixty-five pounds — and this terrific smell of alcohol hits him: Draper was *plastered.*"

"Bubba-*hah!*" Terry Flynn said.

"He'd been sucking up all that home brew he makes in the back of the lab — you ever seen that big whaddyacallit? That big tank, like, with the hose kind of thing sticking out of it? — and he'd gone and fallen all over himself. Jesus, if MacKenzie hadn't of come along he'd of been on his back all night. So MacKenzie puts him into a chair and old Draper looks like he's gonna fall out of that too, and he says 'Please get my wife.' So MacKenzie takes off to the Drapers' house and gets Mrs. Draper — "

"Was she alone?" another voice interrupted. "Was she alone, or was Frenchy La Prade in bed with her?"

"Bubba-*hah!* Bubba-hah-*hah!*" Terry Flynn said.

" — I don't know, I guess she was alone; anyway, the two of 'em manage to get old Draper home and everything, and then Mrs. Draper says to MacKenzie, she says 'This can be just between ourselves, all right?' "

There were a number of English boys at Dorset that year, refugees from the war, and they tended to be favored at faculty teas because of their good manners. One of them was

Richard Edward Thomas Lear, who roomed across the hall
from Terry Flynn. He stood very straight, he had rich black
hair and bright eyes and might have been a handsome boy
except for his mouth, which was as loose and wet as a rooting
animal's.

"You must miss your family terribly," Mrs. Edgar Stone
said to him one October afternoon, leaning over to pour more
tea into his cup. "And I do wish you'd tell me more about
Tunbridge Wells. Has there been much bombing there? I've
just finished reading *The White Cliffs* and I found it wonderfully moving, though of course my husband says it's not a
good book." Mrs. Stone was the scatterbrained wife of the
English master, and this was an important house to visit
because the Stones had a sweet, shy daughter of fifteen
named Edith. She was seldom home, but there was always
a chance. Besides, Mrs. Stone herself wasn't half bad: when
she leaned over with the teapot that way, if you were lucky,
you could get a nice view of ample, creamy breast all the way
down to the nip.

"I hope Tunbridge Wells isn't much changed, Mrs. Stone,"
Richard Edward Thomas Lear said. "I shall want to see it
again as I've remembered it." Then, knocking back his tea,
he stood up. "I'm afraid I must go now. Thanks ever so
much." And when Mrs. Stone turned away to call her husband from the study, Lear reached out one hand, gathered
up six expensive chocolate-dipped cookies and thrust them
into the side pocket of his Dorset blazer.

"Good having you, uh, Lear," Dr. Stone said, blinking in
the doorway.

"It's been a pleasure, sir." Smiling there with one hand
sunk in his blazer pocket, he was the picture of a courteous
departing guest. "Thank you both again."

He ate all the cookies in rapid succession as he walked out

across the quadrangle toward Three building. Upstairs in his
room, feeling a little queasy from the surfeit, he got undressed for his shower. Lear had nothing to fear from the
scrutiny of the shower room: he might not be as spectacular
as Terry Flynn but he was all right, his prick was adequate,
and he had powerful, admirably hairy legs. Another thing:
he knew better than anyone how to snap a wet towel against
the buttocks of other bathers.

Sometimes, though, and particularly at this hour of the
day, an unaccountable melancholy settled on him. He
wanted to punch and wrestle and shout; those were the only
activities that could make him feel fit again. With his shower
completed and his clothes changed for dinner, he went out
into the hall and found Art Jennings intently flicking specks
of lint off his black jacket. Jennings was a hulking, amiable,
nearsighted boy; he was bigger than Lear, but that would
only make it more stimulating.

"My God! Look!" Lear cried in a shocked voice, pointing
dramatically toward the shower room, and when Jennings
turned to look he stepped in and punched him with all his
strength on the upper arm.

"Ow! Son of a *bitch!"* Jennings tried to punch him back
but missed — Lear had stepped out of range and stood smiling there, his wet mouth glistening — and then they were all
over each other, locked in a series of clumsy wrestling holds
as they swayed and fell into Jennings' room. First they were
on the floor, where they knocked over the chair and Jennings' glasses fell off; then they were on the bed, where one
of Lear's flailing feet scraped a long rip in the sailing chart
Jennings had used to decorate his wall. Six or eight other
boys passed the open door and saw them, without much
interest. In the end it was Terry Flynn who broke them up,

as casually as if he were separating two puppies. "C'mon, guys," he said. "That was the three-minute bell."

Gasping for breath, rubbing their sore limbs and necks and ribs, they got dizzily to their feet. Their evening clothes were ruined: one shoulder seam of Lear's jacket was torn out, both their shirts were gray with sweat and their starched collars and bow ties had come absurdly apart. Lying silver on Jennings' lapel was a long, ropy strand of Lear's spit.

"Get you next time, you bastard," Jennings said.

"You and who else?" Lear inquired. He felt marvelous — and Jennings, squinting and fitting his glasses back into place, looked as if he felt good too.

In his second year as French master at Dorset Academy, Jean-Paul La Prade had established an uneasy truce with the place. He would much rather have been back in New York, making ends meet as a translator and occasionally doing what he called "a spot of journalism" — he had been able to stay in bed till noon every day in New York, often with a lively girl — but a man had to change with changing times. The work wasn't hard here, once you'd learned to keep the little bastards off your neck; the pay was wretched but there wasn't anything to spend it on anyway; the daily regimen might be Spartan, but with a little imagination one could manage to live like an adult.

La Prade was thirty-eight. Several girls had called him "wonderfully Gallic" in his New York days, which helped him emphasize his piercing stare and his jaunty short man's gestures and movements; he liked his looks, and tended to strut a little while lecturing his classes. He was fond of his voice, too: it was precise and deep, melodious in encourage-

ment and fearsome in reprimand, with just enough French
accent to give it authority.

"I think it's your voice, as much as anything," Alice Draper had told him last spring. "Your voice, and your eyes, and
the way you touch me — oh, the way you touch me." And
he'd winced at that, because for many years Alice hadn't
been touched by any but the soft, jiggling hands of her pitiable husband. The worst part was that he rather liked poor
Jack Draper; he'd once considered him, in fact, the closest
thing to a friend he had at this funny little school.

Still, Alice had been a good mistress. For a woman of
thirty-six she was remarkably firm in the flesh and remarkably girlish in her eagerness. They had tirelessly writhed
and humped and fed on each other, first in his apartment
(where the pleasure was heightened by their knowledge that
a dormitory packed with kids lay just beyond the steam pipe
overhead) and later on a blanket in the woods. In the woods
one afternoon she had suddenly recoiled from him, covering
her breasts, and pointed to a clumsily running, noisily re-
treating boy who vanished among the trees two hundred feet
away. La Prade had done his best to assure her it didn't
matter, that she mustn't worry about it, but he'd been unset-
tled too. At dinner in the great stone-and-wood refectory that
night he had risked occasional glances up from his plate to
see if anyone in the long, wide sea of kids was looking at him.
Here and there a boy sat silent, lost in loneliness over his
food (and La Prade could understand that; these refectory
meals were a torture). Most of them were turbulent with talk
and laughter — what in God's name did they find so *funny*
all the time? — but even among the heartiest laughers and
nudgers he found no hint of a gaze aimed at himself. Once
he tried discreetly to catch Alice's eye across the room —
he wanted to tell her, with the faintest suggestion of a smile,

that everything would be all right — but she didn't look up.
She wore a severe black dress; there was something strained
about her shoulders and he couldn't see the expression on
her downcast face. At the opposite end of the Drapers' table,
many chattering kids away, poor Jack was wholly engaged
in the difficulty of cutting his meat.

"You'll forget me this summer," Alice had predicted last
June. "You'll have all your old New York girls, and when
you come back in the fall you'll have forgotten you ever had
me."

"Good," he'd said. "That'll make me want to have you all
over again."

But it had been a rotten summer. Living in a dreadful
hotel on upper Broadway, spending too much money on
cheap food, he had failed to find work with any of his old
publishing contacts — and with one exception, a languid
bleached-blonde named Nancy who complained about the
"tackiness" of his room, he had failed to win back any of his
girls. By September, facing another year at Dorset, he'd become preoccupied with Alice. He missed her; he wanted her,
and at the same time he knew he would spend the fall seeking graceful ways to extricate himself. There was no future
in a thing like this.

"Ah, God, how I missed you," she said on their first night
together. "I thought you'd never, ever come back. Did you
miss me?"

"I thought of you all the time."

But now it was November, and common sense made clear
that it couldn't go on. She was nice, but she wanted too
much.

He was alone in his apartment, changing into the darker
of his two suits for dinner, and while knotting his tie at the
mirror he went over some of the things he planned to tell

her. "There's no future in a thing like this," he would say. "I think we've both known that from the beginning. Even if it weren't for Jack, I'd feel — " And his doorbell rang.

Surely she ought to know better than to come here at this time of day. As he hurried across the small space to the front door his irritation dissolved into an invigorating, useful kind of anger: this might be the perfect pretext for the scene he had in mind; he couldn't have asked for a better one.

But it wasn't Alice: it was a gangling, dreary-looking boy of about fifteen. It was William Grove, one of the new boys, the dumbest kid in his fourth-form French class.

"Sir," Grove said, "you told me to come at five-thirty for a conference."

And La Prade almost said "I did?" before he caught himself. Then he said "Right. Come in, Grove; sit down."

The kid was a mess. His tweed suit hung greasy with lack of cleaning, his necktie was a twisted rag, his long fingernails were blue, and he needed a haircut. He seemed in danger of stumbling over his own legs as he made his way to a chair, and he sat so awkwardly as to suggest it might be impossible for his body to find composure. What an advertisement for Dorset Academy!

"I asked you in, Grove," La Prade began, "because I'm worried about you. Here we are in November, and as far as I can tell you haven't learned any French at all. What's the trouble?"

"I don't know, sir."

"Sometimes," La Prade said, "a student will fail at a foreign language because he's deficient in basic verbal skills. But that's clearly not the case with you: Dr. Stone tells me your work in English has been adequate."

"Yes, sir."

"So how do you explain it? How can someone be adequate

in English and wholly incompetent at elementary French?
Mm?"

"I don't know, sir."

The abject way he sat there, head bowed, waiting for his
small ordeal to end, was beginning to get on La Prade's
nerves. "A teacher can do only so much, Grove," he said.
"Teaching is a two-way proposition. No teacher can help a
student who fails to show the slightest — the faintest spark
of comprehension, of willingness to learn. Do you see?"

"No, sir. I mean yes, sir."

La Prade was on his feet now, pacing the small carpet the
way he paced the head of his classroom, one hand jingling
coins in his pocket. This little bastard could be the death of
him. "I have my own theory about you, Grove," he said. "I
think you're lazy. If you weren't lazy you'd clip your fingernails and get a haircut and get your clothes cleaned. You're
adequate in English because you find it easy, and you're
incompetent in French because you find it difficult. And the
point is this, Grove: the point is simply that I won't tolerate
that attitude. You're either going to buckle down or you're
going to — to find yourself in trouble." He was trembling. "Is
that clear?"

"Yes, sir."

"All right. I want five irregular-verb sheets from you by
the end of the week. And they'd better be correct, is that
clear? All right. Go along now."

Watching the boy gather himself up and slink to the door,
he had to hold his jaws shut tight to keep from shouting.
Then Grove was gone, and La Prade was alone with his fists
in his pockets and his breath coming hard through his nose.
It was ridiculous to let the kids upset him this way —
he knew that. The thing to do was relax (That's it, he counselled himself as he sat in his armchair, beginning to breathe

more easily; that's it; just relax) and try to think of what he
would say to Alice tonight.

Darkness had fallen and the big trees were stirring when
William Grove turned the corner into the quadrangle, heading back to Three building. Things could be worse. He had
dreaded his meeting with Frenchy La Prade all day, but it
hadn't been so bad. He would have to do five irregular-verb
sheets by Friday and he wasn't even sure how to do one of
the damn things, but that was something he could worry
about later. The trouble was over for now, and Grove had
learned to be grateful when trouble was over.

"Hey there, Gypsy," said a resonant voice behind him on
the stairway, and he didn't have to turn around to know it
was Larry Gaines, a fifth former and a sure thing for next
year's Student Council, a handsome, athletic boy of seventeen who lived in one of the big rooms on the third floor and
who had addressed several kind, thrillingly friendly remarks to him over the past few weeks. But his pleasure was
quickly spoiled by the voice of Steve MacKenzie, the second-
floor dorm inspector, who was climbing the stairs with
Gaines.

" 'Gypsy'?" MacKenzie inquired. "Whaddya call him
'Gypsy' for?"

"Oh, I don't know," Larry Gaines said. "He sort of reminds
me of a gypsy."

"Yeah? Well, he reminds me of a puddle of piss. Hey there,
Puddle of Piss."

And Grove might have spun around and said "Fuck you,
MacKenzie," but he didn't have that option anymore. He
had done it once last month — he'd turned on him in the hall

and said "Fuck you, MacKenzie," for everyone to hear —
and it had only brought on an impossible situation.

"Well, now," MacKenzie had said, advancing on Grove
with a slow, pleased smile. He wasn't yet sixteen, but he was
enormous. "Well, now. Kind of looks like this little dipshit's
asking for trouble, doesn't it?" With his hands loose at his
sides, he thrust his big face forward. "Wanna take a swing
at me, Grove? Huh? Wanna be a big man and take a swing
at me?"

Grove did take a swing — a hopeless right that missed by
a mile and enabled MacKenzie to seize his arm, turn, crouch,
and throw him over his hip to the floor, to an uproar of
laughter from the crowd. Grove got up, clenched his fists and
tried again, but MacKenzie kept ducking and throwing him
over his hip to the floor until the fun of it wore off. "Oh,
Jesus," he said at last, "will somebody please take this fucking kid away from me before I beat the shit out of him?"

By the standards of most movies he had seen, Grove's
performance that night might have made him a hero, or at
least a scrappy little guy; at Dorset Academy it made him a
fool.

And things hadn't gone much better in his second fight, a
few weeks later, with a wiry French-Canadian kid named
Pete Giroux who lived at the other end of the hall — though
that fight had started, at least, more classically in the Holly-
wood tradition. Giroux, fancying some insult — or pretend-
ing to — had challenged Grove to go to the gym with him.
Grove had accepted, and five or six other boys had gone along
to watch. Even MacKenzie had gone along, to serve as referee and to make sure they all got back before Lights, and
in the gym there were elaborate preparations: tumbling
mats were dragged and fitted together to form a ring; corners
were assigned; a timekeeper was appointed to establish

three-minute rounds. William Grove knew that if he could
do well it might make all the difference — he might still
become a member of this school in good standing — and he
squared off against Giroux with a heartful of hope, but it
didn't work. He tried and tried but couldn't hit Giroux, and
Giroux hit him time and again. They were still in the second
round when they stumbled and fell together; then it became
a wrestling match that Giroux quickly won by twisting
Grove's arm until Grove gave up. Nobody slapped Grove on
the back or said anything nice to him, and all the way back
to the dorm he walked in the grip of a desperate effort to
keep from crying.

He still hadn't cried, except in the privacy of his room late
at night (and even there you couldn't be sure of remaining
alone; the doors were locked only by sliding wooden bolts,
easily picked open with a knife or a screwdriver; nobody was
safe) but he'd come to adopt a chronic posture of humiliation.
If a wretch was what they wanted, he would be a wretch.

"Bubba-*hah!*" Terry Flynn was saying to Richard Edward
Thomas Lear as they walked down to the steaming shower
room together, wearing only their towels. "Bubba-hah-*hah!*"

Big Art Jennings, crouched in his underwear, was shining
his shoes, pausing only to shove his glasses delicately higher
on the bridge of his nose.

John Haskell and Hugh Britt, the two boys on the whole
of the floor with whom Grove wanted most to be friends, sat
engaged in some intellectual discussion in Britt's room. They
were already dressed for dinner — they seemed to do everything well ahead of time. Haskell was homely and said to be
"mature" for his years. He was too awkward for serious
sports but was an excellent student — it was said that he
"challenged" his teachers — and he was managing editor of
the Dorset *Chronicle*. Britt was a new boy, admirably quiet

and self-sufficient, a husky Middle Westerner whose intelligence Haskell seemed to trust. The two of them often sat like this for hours, or walked together among the trees, talking and talking, and everyone else kept a respectful distance.

". . . Well, but it's the *substance* of the thing that matters," Haskell was saying as Grove passed the open door. "Don't you think? Look at it this way . . ."

Alone in his own room, Grove sat on the edge of his bed for a while trying to think of nothing — he often did that — and then began undressing for his shower. When he was naked he gave the head of his prick the ritual tug to make it hang lower, wrapped a towel around himself and walked down the hall into the billowing steam.

The shower room was the worst part of his day. Not only was he absurdly thin and weak-looking, but he hadn't yet developed a full growth of pubic hair: all he had was brown fuzz, and there was no hiding it.

"Here comes Muscles," somebody said when he walked in, to which he replied "Up yours," but except for that they left him pretty much alone.

They left him alone at dinner in the refectory that night too. He ate greedily and heavily, as always, but it caused no banter around the table about his tapeworm. ("How's the old tapeworm, Grove?" somebody'd said once, and that had started it. "Grove, who's *getting* all that stuff — you or the damn tapeworm?" "Know what? Some morning we'll see this *tape*worm come down to breakfast; he'll kind of wriggle up and sit at the table; we'll say 'Where's Grove?' And that old tapeworm'll just sit there looking around with a shit-eating grin . . .")

Haskell and Britt sat talking together, still aloof from the crowd; everyone else on both sides of the long table was engaged in the tireless, self-renewing business of horsing around. They nudged each other frequently, they displayed wide mouthfuls of chewed roast pork and potato and peas when they laughed, sometimes they choked and sputtered on their milk and had to blow their noses thoroughly into their napkins.

Then came the hushed hour-and-a-half of study hall, and Grove found himself unable to get anything done. He started off well enough — he organized all the materials for filling out the first of Frenchy La Prade's irregular-verb sheets (though he would probably have done better to prepare for his history test tomorrow) — but soon he became preoccupied with the sight of his own right hand as it lay palm-down among the books and papers. What bothered him was not its terrible fingernails but that it looked so pale and childish, that its wrist and back held no deeply ridged tracery of veins. Then he found that if he squirmed around and hooked his armpit over the back of his chair, so that the sharp corner of wood bit deeply into the flesh, wrist and hand could be made to swell a little and turn a satisfying shade of dark pink. Heavy veins appeared, even in the backs of the fingers, and the longer he stared at it the better he felt. This was the hand of a man.

"Grove?"

". . . Sir?"

Dr. Edgar Stone was taking study hall that night. He beckoned for Grove to come up and sit beside him; then he said, in a near-whisper appropriate to their surroundings, "What's the trouble, Grove? Aren't you feeling well?"

"No, sir — I mean yes, sir. I was just — I'm all right."

"Do you find it difficult to concentrate?"

"No, sir."

"What're you working on?"

"I don't know, sir. French, mostly."

Dr. Stone looked at him intently for a while before his eyes turned tiredly away, as people's eyes often did after looking at Grove. "All right," he said at last. "Go on back to your desk."

There were almost two hours to kill between study hall and Lights, and this was the time when trouble most often broke out on the second floor of Three building.

". . . Oh, Jesus, that little Edith Stone," somebody was saying in the hall.

"Yeah? Edith Stone? She home?"

"Whaddya, blind? Didn'tcha see her at dinner? She was sitting at the Stones' *table,* for Christ's sake."

"Yeah? I didn't see her."

"You wouldn't see her if she shoved her pussy in your face."

"I got something to shove in *your* face . . ."

". . . No, but listen, though, *I* got an idea: Get Grove, strip him bare-assed, tie him up, carry him over and put him on the Stones' doorstep, ring the bell and take off."

"Bubba-*hah!*"

William Grove, alone in his room when he heard this, looked over to make sure the wooden bolt of his door was closed. It was, but to take no chances he got up and stood holding it shut with both hands.

Soon the talk in the hall went on to other things — apparently he wasn't in danger after all — and he began to feel foolish for standing here in an attitude of grim self-protection. Being "brave" hadn't won him anything, but hiding like a coward was worse.

". . . You're fulla shit," somebody was saying now. "Whaddya mean, he threw a pass sixty yards? Nobody in this *school* can throw a pass sixty yards . . ."

". . . And so anyway, I said 'Look, sir, you didn't give us *time* to cover three chapters,' and he said . . ."

That was how the talk was going — aimless, harmless — when Grove let himself out into the hall. He intended to join one of the groups of talkers as discreetly as possible — not as a participant, necessarily, but as an amiable listener: an oddball, maybe, but nonetheless one of the guys.

Richard Edward Thomas Lear saw him coming. "Grove," he said. "I say, Grove, how're you feeling tonight?" His wet smile glistened.

"Okay."

"Feeling okay, are you? Good. Grove is feeling okay. I say, everyone — " He raised his voice to address the hall. "May I have your attention, please? I have an announcement to make. Grove is feeling okay tonight."

"Up yours, Lear," Grove said, but his voice was lost under the clamor of advancing boys. They were all over him in a second, four or five of them, sweeping him easily off his feet and carrying him. He thrashed his arms and legs, hitting someone under the chin; then all his limbs were caught and held and he rode helpless in their grip.

"Bubba-hah-*hah!*"

They had started up the hall as if heading for the stairs — good God, were they going through with the plan to leave him naked on the Stones' doorstep?—but then, well short of the stairs, they stopped and turned and carried him into Art Jennings' room. They laid him sideways on the bed, removed his shoes, unbuckled his belt and pulled off his pants. He worked one foot free and kicked with it, but it was quickly caught and twisted; then Art Jennings straddled him, facing his feet, and sat on his face.

Under the stifling weight of wool-clad buttocks he could no longer see, but he could hear. ". . . Shaving cream," somebody was saying, and somebody else said "Call that hair? Shit, you could *wipe* it off." He felt warm water around his groin and the careful scrape of a safety razor; it didn't take long.

But the shaving turned out to be only a preliminary action. When it was done he felt a hand close around his prick — and whose hand was that? Which of these bastards was queer enough to take somebody else's prick in his hand? — and begin the rhythmic work of masturbation.

". . . Hey, now you're getting it; *now* it's coming up . . ."

And this was true: Grove was getting a hard-on, in spite of himself. Quick taunting visions of girls' naked breasts, of girls' naked thighs and crotches swam in the seat of Art Jennings' pants, and Grove knew he would be utterly helpless in a spasm of release at any moment now, unless he fought for control.

And so he fought for control. It took all the power of concentration he could never bring to his studies, but he won.

". . . Ah, shit, it's going down. You lost it . . ."

They hadn't jerked him off; they hadn't made him come, and he knew now that they wouldn't. It might be a dismal triumph, but it was a kind of triumph all the same. Then Jennings shifted his weight, moving from Grove's face to somewhere below his throat, and by squirming and craning around Grove could see the hand that still worked on him. Its little-finger was elegantly stiff: it was Terry Flynn.

It took some seconds for Grove to realize that his mouth was free; he could shout now, and he did: "Fuck you! Fuck you! Fuck you! . . ."

"Shut him up; he'll get Driscoll up here."

Flynn's hand was still pumping — he wouldn't give up, and he frowned soberly over his task — but Grove felt he had outwitted them all. Except for the shaved hair it couldn't even be said that they'd humiliated him; the whole episode might still be written off as a dormitory prank, and to encourage that view he began laughing artificially and shouting through his laughter: "Yeah, yeah, keep trying, you sonsabitches, keep trying — wow, are *you* guys ever having yourselves a good time. Go ahead, try! Try a little harder! . . ."

He was still shouting and laughing — looking, probably, the picture of depravity — when John Haskell and Hugh Britt came strolling past the open door. Haskell looked down at Flynn's laboring hand with an embarrassed smile; Britt glanced at Grove's face, and his own face winced as if he'd smelled something rancid.

MacKenzie called "Lights!" then; Grove was set free and ran to his room, and for hours after that, alone in the darkness, he lay wondering how he was going to live the rest of his life.

Chapter 2

The news of Pearl Harbor seemed to have little effect on Dorset Academy for a few weeks; then the changes began.

Speaking in his most solemn tones at assembly, W. Alcott Knoedler announced a new program of "wartime discipline." He didn't make clear exactly what this would entail, beyond an increase in the community-service workload, a more austere diet, and the need to black-out all windows during air-raid drills, but he managed to imbue it with a spirit of sacrifice. "Our nation is at war," he said, "and we will conduct ourselves accordingly."

The Alumni News column of the Dorset *Chronicle* became filled to overflowing with reports of military assignments,

and soon there was even a death: someone from the class of
'38 had been killed in the Pacific.

Harold "Choppy" Tyler, the athletic director, designed
and built what he insisted on calling a "commando course"
in the woods behind the refectory. It was finished by early
spring, and everyone in the three upper forms was required
to go through it once a day. First you dropped into a chin-
deep foxhole and had to scramble out, then came a high
wooden wall that you had to scale (some boys went over it
easily, others had to hang trembling by the hands or armpits
until they managed to work one foot over the top, still others
sneaked around it when Choppy wasn't looking). There were
ropes to climb and parallel bars to negotiate, and at the end
there was a low tunnel roofed with chickenwire that you had
to crawl through like a snake.

Choppy Tyler would stand near the starting line, a short,
massive, humorless man described as "muscle-bound" by the
boys, and blow his whistle to send them off two at a time.
Between heats, with the whistle silent on its thong against
his sweatshirt, he would cup both hands to his mouth and
call things like "You kids think *this* is rough, wait'll you get
in the *Army.*"

Robert Driscoll, the assistant English master and school
disciplinarian, would sometimes come out and stand beside
him to watch the boys go through the course.

"Think they're getting the hang of it, Chop?" he asked one
afternoon.

"Some of 'em are," Tyler said. "A few of 'em are, but most
of 'em are still goofing off."

"Well, it's bound to take a little time."

Except that his eyes looked startled when he took off his
glasses, everything about Robert Driscoll suggested balance.
His thick, wiry hair might have been hard to control if he let

it grow, so he kept it short. His lean face was broad in the
jaw, and his mouth gave shape to the quality of fairness.

A prep school teacher was all he had ever wanted to be.
The ambition had come to him during his own student days
at Deerfield (where he'd set two records in track that remained unbroken to this day), and it hadn't wavered at
Tufts. He had started his career in a small New Jersey school
that went under in the Depression; then he'd had to sell
insurance for a living until 1937, when he heard that a new
man named Knoedler was hiring a new staff at a place called
Dorset Academy. Knoedler was said to be the fourth headmaster in twelve years — that didn't sound too good —
but other things about the school were promising, or at least
challenging; besides, what did he have to lose?

He had lost nothing, and it seemed to him now that he'd
gained a great deal. At forty, he was the most respected and
the most popular man on the Dorset faculty. He and his wife
were called "Pop" and "Mom" by the boys, and it pleased
him to think of this place as the setting for the rest of their
lives.

"No, *no,*" Choppy Tyler was calling. "You gotta *hit* that
wall. You can't go creeping up on it like some girl or something, you gotta *hit* it." But then a couple of fifth formers
went over the wall nicely, making it shudder, showing a lot
of hustle as they bore down on the next obstacle, and
Choppy's face went solemn with satisfaction.

"Well," Robert Driscoll said. "I'll see you, Chop."

"See you, Bob." And two other kids were able to sneak
around the wall as Choppy turned to watch Driscoll walk
away. With the wet whistle poised at his chin, he was envi-
ously studying the way Driscoll's tweed jacket seemed to
encase his shoulders like an agreeable second skin, without
the slightest hint of stretch or bulge. However Choppy Tyler

held himself in three-way mirrors, however he quarrelled
with the little men who made the alterations, he could never
get his own coats to fit and hang like that.

Robert Driscoll often assured himself that Dorset Academy was a good school; even so, there was a nagging qualification: if only it were more like a *real* school. And almost
everyone else here seemed to carry that sense of inauthen-
ticity around with them — the faculty, the boys — you could
see it in their faces.

For one thing, whoever heard of a school that didn't field
varsity teams in competition with other schools? Wasn't that
the very heart of prep school life? But because of a peevish
stipulation in the crazy old lady's charter (and that, of
course, was another thing: whoever heard of a school whose
charter had been written by a crazy old lady?) they were
isolated. They were stuck with intramural sports. The Eagles played the Beavers every week, and that was that. In
football season, since there weren't enough players for regu-
lation teams, they played six-man football — a center and
two ends, a three-man backfield. It was a fast game and
sometimes lively to watch, but it was a sloppy game too, with
far too many touchdowns.

The boys were nice enough about it, for the most part; they
did their best to cultivate a sense of loyalty and pride as
Eagles or Beavers, and when the scores were announced
after dinner their cheers rang heartily from the big refectory
walls; but Driscoll, stirring his coffee under the tumult of
that cheering, would often think No, no; this isn't right. This
isn't right.

All he could do — all anyone could do — was hope for
growth and change and improvement in the future. And

certainly the materials for a real school were here; the "physical plant" was here; you had to hand it to the old lady for that. Walking now along the side of the refectory he decided once again, as he often did, that this was probably the best single view of the campus. From here you could see a whole sweep, a whole intricate frieze of the school's lovely "Cotswold" architecture. It began with a quaint little cluster of low-roofed buildings where the guest house and the post office were, it moved across the long, stern façade of the Council hall to the dean's office, then on around the curve of the wide flagstone path to the archway of Three building, which formed the rear of the quadrangle; and on the other side of that curve, set apart on its own lawn, lay the handsome structure of the headmaster's residence.

Still, there were other views. He could never make the drive back from Hartford without admiring the way the school looked as it was meant to be seen for the first time: you came around the side of the enormous water tower and there it was, three hundred yards straight ahead down the broad red driveway. There stood One building, with the stout little squared-off tower above its archway, and there, off to the right in the trees, was a partial view of smaller buildings promising other fine things to be discovered.

Then sometimes during duck-hunting season, when he came trudging home for breakfast up the steep wooded hill below Two building, he would stop with the broken-open shotgun in his elbow and wonder if this might not be the most dramatic view of all — the high glistening monolith of Two building, all stone and slate, looming out of the morning mist like a medieval fortress.

Occasionally, on warm Sunday afternoons, he would take a pad of drawing paper out on the grass and try to capture some of his feeling for the place in charcoal. He never tried for much — the play of sun and shadow in an archway, say, or a receding row of slate-gabled windows, or a juncture of chimney-top and roofline against the trees — but even when his wife called some of the sketches "beautiful" he knew he had failed. The essence of a beloved place was as elusive as that of a beloved person — and he'd tried to capture that too, long ago, when he and Marge were first married. He'd made many charcoal drawings of her sweet young face, and many more, despite her blushing objections, of her achingly sweet young body in the nude, but he'd thrown them all away.

He was walking past the Council hall when its heavy doors opened and ten or twelve men came out. They were men he didn't know — all wearing dark business suits, some carrying briefcases — and he came to a stop and backed off on the edge of the path, ready to smile in case any of them should smile at him, but they swept past him without a glance. Only when he saw W. Alcott Knoedler emerge chatting among the last of them did he realize that this had been a meeting of the board of trustees. They would hurry around through the Three building archway now and out across the quadrangle to their waiting cars in front of One building; they'd disperse to Hartford and Boston and New York with the destiny of Dorset Academy in their hands.

He waited until Knoedler had finished shaking hands with the last trustee; then he went up to him and said "How'd it go, Alcott?"

"Oh, not well, Bob." Knoedler's face was still tense with the effort of his official smile. "Not really well at all, but better than I'd feared." Slowly, as his eyes came into focus on Driscoll, he began to relax in the knowledge that the board meeting was over. "Better than I'd feared," he said again, "and perhaps in some ways better than I'd dared hope. Do you have a minute, Bob? Want to come over to the office?"

When he was settled behind his big desk Knoedler turned away and opened one panel of the oaken wall behind him, disclosing a little cupboard from which he removed a tray with a decanter of sherry and several glasses.

". . . the operating deficit," he was saying. "Bob, I can't tell you how tired I am of hearing about the operating deficit. It's all these people want to talk about. You'd think we were running a factory. Well; cheers." He took a sip of sherry and set his glass down carefully on the desk blotter. "And of course our operating deficit *is* alarming, but I keep trying to explain there are things that can be done. And I think I did manage to get a few points across this afternoon. I told them . . ."

With the sherry warm and pleasant on his tongue, Driscoll sat back and let the words drift past his hearing. In no sense did Alcott Knoedler fit the role of a "beloved" headmaster; nobody loved him. It was partly that he spent almost half his time away from school, on the road, following up letters of inquiry from parents of prospective Dorset boys, "drumming up trade," as he liked to say at faculty meetings. But even if he'd stayed home he probably wouldn't have kindled much affection: he was a chilly man, a devious man, a talking, smiling, public-relations man, and the boys referred to him as Old Bottle-ass because he was tall and fragile-looking, with a high waist and wide hips. Possibly no man built like that could hope to cut much of a figure in a boys' school. Nor could his wife do anything to help his career: she might once have been a pleasant and pretty girl, but now her face was forever set in a numb smile, as if injected in many places with Novocain. Other faculty wives said you could know her for years without hearing her say anything but "So nice; so nice."

". . . and so you see it's Mrs. Hooper again," Knoedler was saying, "always, always Mrs. Hooper. Even after she dies that charter of hers will have the school hamstrung for years to come, and her being very much with us, ten miles away, only makes matters worse. She's either eighty-two or eighty-four now, and she's what any qualified physician would call senile. She won't be reasoned with, won't be reasoned with, and I must say it sometimes seems she has all the trustees in her pocket. In any case, the charter hems us in on every side. Well" — and here he ventured a little smile as he swirled the sherry in his glass — *"almost* every side. I've learned that when the financial picture gets bleak enough, *some* questions can be raised. I think I made some fairly good inroads today on the question of dress."

"Oh?"

"Oh, I can't promise anything yet, but wouldn't it be good to tell them they can wear their own clothes next year? No more uniforms, no more monkey-suits and stiff collars at night?"

"Well, sure," Driscoll said, putting his empty glass on the desk, "it's just that I still think — you know — I still think the major issue is interscholastic sports."

"And you're by no means alone in that," Knoedler said. "I agree with you, and I hear the same thing everywhere I go. Well." He stood up, causing Driscoll to stand up too, and came around the desk to offer his hand. He had a surprisingly firm handshake; he had probably learned on the road that a good grip meant business. "Well," he said again as he walked his guest to the door. "We'll get there yet, Bob. One thing at a time."

And Driscoll was out under the trees again, heading home.
He had just started up the path to the Three building archway when a group of the bigger kids came jogging up from
behind and overtook him, winded and laughing, on their way
back from the commando course. One of them was Larry
Gaines, who dropped away from the others as they passed
and fell into step with him.

"Been through the course yet, Pop?"

"I'm waiting for Mr. Knoedler, Larry. I'm ready whenever
he is."

"Wow, wouldn't that be something to see?" Larry Gaines
said. "The two of you hitting the wall together? Listen, be
sure and let me know when you do it, okay? I want to get a
camera."

"They got you playing first base for the Eagles this year,
Larry?"

"I don't know; been thinking I might go out for track."

"Good," Driscoll said. "Good."

"Will you be coaching the milers again?"

"I hope to be."

"Good. Because I'd really like to try the mile."

"Well, good; that'll be good."

"Good."

They were both aware of having said "good" too many
times, and it made them chuckle foolishly and look down at
the flagstones. They had come to a stop inside the heavily
shadowed archway now, and Larry stood with most of his
weight on the raddled sneaker of one foot, his thumbs
hooked in his jeans. "Well," he said at last, looking up and
smiling. "See you, sir."

The boys called Driscoll "Pop" but they called him "sir"
too; he had to admit he liked that. And he had to admit,
moving out into the quadrangle, that this wasn't the first

time he had come away blushing and pleasurably embarrassed from a small conversation with Larry Gaines. What
was it about that kid? He was a top student, for one thing,
and a good athlete — not great, not what could be called a
natural, but good enough for any varsity football team that
Dorset might field in the future (and wouldn't it be good if
he turned out to be a good miler too?) — and it was clear now
that he'd be elected to the Student Council next year and
would almost certainly be its President, the highest of all
student offices. But when you'd said all that you had only
begun to describe Larry Gaines; there was much more. He
was so *nice*. There was nothing of the campus politician
about him, ingratiating himself with other kids to win votes;
he was just considerate and kind and nice to almost everyone. And he was — well, it might sound funny to say aloud,
but he was just about the best-looking boy in the school.
Looking into his bright face could make you almost as shy
as looking into the face of a beautiful girl.

The quadrangle was crawling with kids at this time of day;
they were coming back to the dorms to take showers. Some
of them called to one another across the wide space, and
their blurred cries of greeting and teasing and reproach
echoed up into the trees.

The second floor of Two building was where the little kids
lived, the first and second formers, and Driscoll felt a stirring
of uneasiness when he glanced over at that particular line
of windows. His only child, Bobby, who with dizzying sudden-
ness had become thirteen years old, was now in residence up
there as a member of the second form. Bobby was overweight
and his teeth needed straightening; worse, he seemed to like
to play the fool, the kind of kid most other kids find silly and
tiresome. Marge had insisted on letting him live at home
during his first-form year, and that had probably been a

mistake: he simply hadn't yet learned how to act right; how
to handle himself; how to get along.

Still, there was plenty of time. A lot of kids went through
an awkward age. Bobby would grow and change and develop,
and meanwhile Driscoll knew it was wrong to worry about
him. The worry, if it showed, would only compound the
trouble.

Besides, it was too nice an afternoon, too sweet a time of
year to worry about anything. The subtle, smoky taste of
Knoedler's sherry lingered with him as he walked, and so did
the benediction of Larry Gaines' smile. Marge would be back
from Hartford by now; she would have her purchases displayed in the living room ("Do you really like it, Bob? I did
think it was a bargain because I got it on sale, and I thought
it might go well with . . ."). And as she talked and moved
around the room in that happy, home-from-shopping mood
she would absently wipe a short lock of hair from her brow
with one finger, a pointless little gesture that could sometimes make his throat ache with tenderness.

The remarkable thing about Marge was that she was still
a girl. Oh, she was mature and responsible and all the other
things a woman of her age was supposed to be, but she hadn't
lost that shy young freshness. Even after all these years of
marriage he thought of her as a girl, and never more so than
when they were in bed. It wasn't just that she felt as slender
and firm as ever; it was that her little shoulders, her narrow
back and limbs looked almost adolescent, almost childish, so
that when she turned to let him take her in his arms —
especially when she turned slowly, with a pout of desire on
her pretty face — there was always a sweet surprise in her
offering of real, grown-up woman's breasts, and then of a big,
proud, grown-up woman's bush coming up at the juncture of
her thighs. Ripe sensuality arising out of innocence —

that was the quality he had tried and tried to catch in those foolish charcoal drawings long ago; that was what had filled him, as a bridegroom, with the wish that there were some final authority, some arbiter, some God to whom he might go and say "Do you mean this marvelous creature is *mine?* Do you mean I can *have* her?"

And it was only five o'clock in the afternoon. He would go home and approve of all the things she'd bought, he would smile and nod as she talked and he'd fix them a couple of drinks; then he'd look at her long and hard and move up close and kiss her on the mouth. She had worn her blue jersey dress today, and he knew how that particular fabric felt sliding under his hands against her back; it felt like sex itself. And maybe she'd laugh and try to fend him off but he knew she liked it in the afternoons — they had agreed long ago that afternoons were even better than nights — and he would take her upstairs and have her. He would have her and have her, while the big trees stirred and rustled new leaves beyond the windows, and she'd say "Oh, Bob; oh, Bob . . ." and the sky would turn from blue to red to black and they'd miss dinner, and they wouldn't care.

Bobby lay sprawled on the living room sofa, eating a marshmallow. That was the first thing he saw when he let himself into the house, and he said "What's this? Why aren't you up in the dorm?"

"Aw, gee, Dad, I'm only — "

"And don't give me 'Aw, gee, Dad,'" Driscoll said. The harshness of his own voice surprised him, but he couldn't stop. "If you want to be a member of the second form you've got to *be* a member of the second form. You've got to — "

"Bob!"

Only then did he realize Marge was in the room. She was

standing at a chair filled with department-store boxes and wrappings, and there was sudden anger in her face. "I won't have you *railing* at him," she said.

"I'm not 'railing'; I'm simply saying he ought to be up in the dorm and he knows that as well as I do, and so do you. He isn't supposed to *live* here anymore, Marge."

And without raising her voice — she almost never raised her voice — she said "Will you calm down, please? Will you try to control yourself? He came over because I asked him to, so he could try on the jeans and the sweatshirts I bought in town. Now; don't you feel foolish?"

He did; he certainly did, and there was no way to laugh it off. But he wasn't quite ready to apologize, either, so all he said was "Okay; okay." After a while he said "Any mail?"

"Nothing much. It's there on the table."

There were only bills and a magazine, but fingering through them gave him something to do.

Sometimes, trying to see his son as others did, Driscoll was encouraged to believe that Bobby wasn't really fat, that the teeth and the braces didn't really spoil his mouth, that his face showed signs of intelligence and humor and manliness, but this wasn't one of those times. Bobby hadn't stirred from his heavy collapse on the sofa. He lay staring at nothing, and there was a fine dust of confectioner's sugar on his petulant lips.

Turning away from him, Driscoll looked shyly at his wife. "Did you — drive in alone today?" he inquired. "Or with Alice?"

"With Alice. We had lunch at the Drake." She was folding paper bags and flattening boxes, and she sounded tired but didn't sound mad at him anymore. She never stayed mad for long; she was, in fact, a girl in whom anger never seemed very convincing in the first place. "I got those slipcovers I

told you about," she was saying, "and a couple of dresses
— one of them I think I'll take back. Oh, and I looked at a
few raincoats, for you, but they were terribly expensive."

"That's okay," he assured her, "my raincoat's okay."

So it was turning into almost as nice a homecoming as he'd
planned, after all. When she carried out the store wrappings
he followed her into the kitchen, noticing the shift and float
of the blue jersey skirt, and did his best to keep the good
mood going. "I feel sort of like having a martini," he said.
"Don't you? Do we have any gin?"

"I don't think so."

There was no liquor at all in the cabinet except an inch of
dry vermouth in a cloudy green bottle. "Oh," he said. "Well,
it doesn't matter." And he went to the refrigerator to look
for beer, but there was no beer either.

After a moment he went over to the counter near the
drainboard and hitched himself up onto it, one foot dangling.
"You know," he said, "I really like that dress of yours. I
always have."

"Oh?" And instead of looking up into his eyes she looked
down at the dress. "Well," she said, "it's as old as God."

Bobby had left the sofa when they went back into the
living room; he was over near the far wall, keeping his distance, fooling around with a fielder's glove. He would repeatedly sock his fist into its pocket and then stand with his feet
well apart, squinting along his left shoulder with the glove
and the imaginary ball nestled close to his chest in a fairly
good imitation of what real pitchers do when they're holding
a man on first. At nine and ten and eleven he had done
things like this for hours, lost in fantasy, sometimes audibly
whispering to himself.

But he seemed to tire of it quickly now. He put the glove
away in the closet under the stairs, where Marge kept a lot

of his belongings, and came toward her across the carpet. "Hey, Mom?" he said. "Be okay if I take a shower here?"

And that did it for Driscoll. Days and even hours later he was able to acknowledge the innocence of the question, but at the time no power on earth could have held back his rage.

"No," he said. "No, it would *not* be okay. You're going to pick up your stuff, right now, and you're going to go up to the dorm and take your shower with the other boys. If you're ashamed to get undressed in front of the other boys that's not at all surprising, and it's regrettable, but maybe it's something you ought to think about the next time you want to lie around stuffing yourself with *marsh*mallows all day."

Bobby's eyes seemed to have gone out of focus. He was just standing there and taking it; and Marge, over by the fireplace, didn't look angry this time. It was worse: she looked hurt — stunned and waiting for the pain to start — and she looked older than her age.

Driscoll sat down, taking off his glasses, and rubbed his eyes hard and slowly with his fingers. After a while he said "I'm sorry, Marge," but she didn't say anything.

With the new jeans and sweatshirts folded over his arm, Bobby walked to the front door. When he opened it Driscoll called, softly, "Bobby?"

The boy turned back, but they didn't quite look at each other.

"I'm sorry, son," Driscoll said.

Much later that night, when he left the house carrying a flashlight in one hand and a clipboard in the other, to make his rounds, Driscoll was able to assure himself that it hadn't been too bad. He had managed to make it up with Marge — not in the way he would have liked to, but they'd had what he now considered a good talk. The only unfortunate part had been at the end, when she'd said she was too tired to wait up for him.

"Oh? How come?"

"What do you mean, 'how come'? I'm *tired*, that's all."

Things would be all right in the morning — he was certain of that — and time would settle it all out.

There was rarely anything out of the ordinary to be dealt with on his nightly rounds: he would proceed counter-clockwise around the quadrangle, and at each stairway landing a dorm inspector would be waiting to say "Everything okay, Pop," or "Everything okay, sir." Some of them were more reliable than others — he never felt wholly comfortable with MacKenzie, for instance, on the second floor of Three building; there was something a little shifty about MacKenzie's face, suggesting that perhaps he shouldn't have been appointed a dorm inspector in the first place — but in general the rounds were a time of peace and satisfaction.

And that was the way it went tonight: everything was so thoroughly okay in all the dorms that he found himself standing for a long time around the Four building archway, fiddling with his flashlight, wondering how best to kill the hour or two before he could sleep.

Only half of Four building's dormitory space was used for that purpose — the school hadn't yet achieved a large enough enrollment to fill it — but now the other half had come to serve as quarters for the kitchen help, since the gasoline shortage made it no longer possible to bring them out from Hartford and back each day. There were six or eight of them, gaunt, solitary-looking men in stained white cotton. They were at work before anyone else was up in the morning, but you could see them walking home at dusk, one at a time, slow with fatigue, cupping roll-your-own Bull Dur-

ham cigarettes in their hands. Driscoll had been a little
uneasy about this Four building arrangement at first —
boys did tend to romanticize the lives of characters like that
— and the uneasiness must have been general, because the
barracks were sealed-off from the rest of the school with
heavy plywood partitions and locks, but nobody needed to
have worried. The boys behaved as if the kitchen help didn't
exist, and the kitchen help kept entirely to themselves. It
occurred to Driscoll to wonder sometimes what they must
think of this place as they sat hunched in their underwear
on their bunks upstairs, looking out over the quadrangle,
putting themselves to sleep with bottles of cheap wine in
paper bags.

Well, the world was funny; nobody had ever said it wasn't.
And he was walking again now, beginning to feel a nice
tingle of expectation, because he had decided it wasn't too
late to drop in on the Drapers for a drink.

By daylight, the sandy area out behind Four building was
the only drab part of the campus. Crazy old Mrs. Hooper had
originally planned on a school twice this size, and partial
foundations had been laid for a second quadrangle that
would have stood here. They were like long, low ruins of an
ancient place, those unfinished foundations; they jarred your
sense of symmetry; they cluttered the view on your way to
the infirmary, or over to the science building and the Drapers' house. And at night, if you weren't careful, you could
stumble over the masonry.

In the distance the Drapers' kitchen windows blazed with
light — good; they were up — and for a few moments Driscoll allowed his thoughts to dwell on what he planned to do
in school tomorrow. "Oh, it's 'Tommy this' and 'Tommy
that,' " he recited just under his breath as he walked, "and
'Tommy, stay outside,' but it's 'Special train for Atkins'

when the troopship's on the tide . . ." He had taken his
fifth-form class through any number of English poets this
year, starting with Donne; all fall and winter they had
drowsed in the tedium of verse that took an effort of will to
read, let alone to understand, but now it was spring; they
were well into the nineteenth century, and tomorrow he
would introduce them to Kipling. "Then it's 'Tommy this'
and 'Tommy that,' and 'Tommy, 'ow's your soul?' But it's
'Thin red line of 'eroes' when the drums begin to roll."

He knew they'd like it. Oh, bless their hearts, he knew
they'd like it, and he knew they'd like the way he read it
aloud. It was more than a little appropriate for them, too:
their own troopships would be on the tide soon enough; the
drums were beginning to roll for them now.

Jack Draper was sitting alone at the bright kitchen table.
Driscoll saw that through the panes of the kitchen door as
he rang the bell; then he saw him look up and smile and go
through the slow procedure of getting to his feet and coming
forward. "Hello, Bob," he said. "Good to see you. Come on
in."

"I know it's late," Driscoll said. "I just thought I'd drop by
in case you were still up. Alice in bed?"

"No, she's — out," Draper said. "Pull up a chair. Here, let
me get you a drink."

It soon became clear, as Driscoll took small sips of the
powerful highball set before him, that Draper must have
been boozing here for some time. He wasn't drunk, exactly,
but he had drunk himself into the kind of expansive mood
that made him apt to say the first crazy thing that came into
his head.

". . . No, but seriously," he was saying. "Seriously, Bob,
have you ever stopped to consider what a tremendous
amount of sheer sexual energy we're harboring here? Espe-

cially at this time of night? Just imagine what we'd find if we could make those big stone dormitory walls fall away: a hundred and twenty-five kids all beating their meat at once."

And Driscoll laughed — it *was* pretty funny — but when Draper's voice started up again, building toward the next laugh, he glanced out into the shadowed hallway beyond the kitchen and turned quickly back with one forefinger against his lips, saying "Sh-sh."

Millicent Draper came in, seven years old, shading her eyes against the brightness. Her rich tan hair was rumpled from bed; she was wearing what looked like a brand-new cotton nightgown, and she carried a very old stuffed animal that could have been either a dog or a bear.

All the drink seemed to vanish from Jack's face and voice. "Well," he said. "Hello, lovey."

"Daddy? Mommy said we could each have a cookie if we woke up."

"Well, then, I guess you'd better go and get one. Can you reach them?"

"Yes."

"Did Jeff wake up too?"

"Yes."

"Then I guess you'd better get two. Have we been talking too loud down here?"

"No," she said, "we just woke up anyway."

Draper watched her as she moved through the kitchen. Then he said "Wow. That certainly is a nice-looking night-gown. Is that one of the nightgowns Mommy bought in Hartford today? With Mrs. Driscoll?"

"Yes. The other one's pink and the other one's blue."

When she was ready to leave he turned partly away from the table and said "How about a hug?"

And she gave him a good one, both arms going up and around his neck, both wrists turned back to accommodate the animal and the cookies. The sight of Jack Draper's crippled hands pressed against her back brought a sweet rush of pain to Driscoll's eyes and throat. He wished he had a daughter.

When she was gone Draper sat looking at his drink for a while; then he glanced over and saw that Driscoll's glass was empty. "Help yourself, Bob," he said. "Here, wait, I'll get you some ice." And he began the struggle to stand up.

"No, really," Driscoll said, "I'd better get home."

"Sit still."

"Well, okay, one more. But hell, let me get the ice, Jack."

"Sit *still*, I said." He sounded angry, making his way to the refrigerator, and he added "I can do *some* things." Then came the clatter of an ice tray in the sink and the hiss of hot water running over it, while Driscoll sat feeling apologetic. It wasn't easy to know how to behave with a handicapped person.

"So where were we?" Draper demanded when he was settled at the table again. "Oh, yes. Sexual energy. What we're harboring here." And he took a long drink. "Well, old man, I don't suppose I'm telling you anything you don't know, or haven't heard, or haven't guessed, but the fact is we're harboring a short little rat-faced bastard here whose sexual energy knows no bounds, and of course it wouldn't do to reveal his identity, but his name is Frenchy Fucking La Prade."

"I don't get it," Driscoll said.

"You don't get it? Why not? Everybody *else* seems to get it, all the way down to about the kids in the third form — you oughta see the way those little buggers look at me all day. Come on, Driscoll, don't be dense. Where the hell do you

think she *is* tonight? Where do you think she's been damn
near every night since way back last spring when I was too
dumb to know what the hell was going on?"

It broke over Driscoll in little waves of incredulity —
Alice *Draper?* Frenchy La *Prade?* — and then the worst
thing was that he didn't know what to say. He was afraid he
might be blushing. "Well, Jack," he said at last, "I had no
idea you were going through something like this."

And Draper looked wretched now, probably hating himself for having divulged it. "Yeah, well, it hasn't been very
jolly," he said. "Sometimes I think I'd rather be dead."

"You don't mean that. You know you don't mean that."

When he'd first met the Drapers, Driscoll had performed
a secret little arithmetic problem in his head, and now he did
it again, just to make sure. Jack had been stricken with polio
when he was twenty-nine, the year after his marriage. He
was thirty-eight now; Millicent was seven and Jeff was five,
and that proved the disease hadn't affected his reproductory
system.

Then he was confronted by what seemed a significant
moral question: should he tell Marge about this? And he had
just resolved that he wouldn't — a thing like this was much
better kept to himself — when it occurred to him that Marge
might already know. She and Alice could easily have discussed it at length on those drives into Hartford, or over
their chicken salad at the Drake hotel, and maybe Marge
had decided to keep it from *him*. Well, but why would she
want to do that?

"Listen, Jack," he said, leaning across the table, and he
would have clasped Draper's arm if he hadn't been afraid to
find out how thin it was. "Listen: I don't understand women
any better than you do, but you can't let yourself go to pieces

over this. You've got to take care of yourself, that's the main thing now. You've got to take care of yourself."

"Thanks, old friend," Draper said in a flat voice, "but you're missing the point. I've been taking exquisitely good care of myself for years. All cripples do."

Dining tables occupied only half the refectory; the other half, the far end of it, was used as the assembly area. Every day, at the chime of a small table bell after the lunch dishes were cleared away, the entire student body and faculty would rise and move, heavy with food, to the rows of folding steel chairs that stood facing a speaker's podium against the far wall. The faculty sat in the rear, and the boys were ranked ahead of them from the sixth form down, with the little kids in front. Knoedler always made the day's announcements when he was home — any of several other masters took over when he was gone — and he liked to make a little drama out of them: he would start off with unimportant things and save the big stuff for the end. When there wasn't any big stuff, which was most of the time, he would contrive to give his final announcement the sound of something more important than it was; sometimes too, as a change of pace, he would save some comic item for last, though he usually spoiled those jokes by telegraphing them with a sly little smile.

From his bearing at the podium one Monday in April, as he neared the climax of his performance, everyone could tell it was the most ordinary of days: there would be no big stuff, no funny stuff, probably nothing even Knoedler could dramatize.

"Three weeks ago," he said, "I announced a contest for essays under the general title *America at War,* to be judged by Dr. Stone, for which first prize would be appointment to the editorial staff of the Dorset *Chronicle*. The results of that contest are now final, and I have the names of the winners here. First prize has been awarded to William Grove of the fourth form."

The applause was only mild, but it struck William Grove as astonishing that there should be any applause at all. He sat hunched in his chair, determined not to smile or to turn either right or left, and he was so concerned with his own appearance that he didn't catch the names of the second- and third-prize winners, though he noticed they were both in the higher forms.

When he got up and faced the aisle to file out with the rest of the audience, he found he had developed a strange new ability to see himself whole, from the outside, as if through a movie camera twenty feet away. He could observe all his gestures — the drawing-back of his coat for the placing of one hand in his pocket, the slight straightening of his spine and lifting of his chin — and the movie camera went right along with him, back through the refectory and out into the sunshine.

He knew he ought to hurry to the dorm because this was a community-service day, rather than a sports day; he would spend the afternoon in his work clothes, riding around in a pickup truck with three or four other kids to clear brush or haul trash under the guidance of a disgruntled school employee, and the truck was probably waiting for them now. But he took his time anyway, strolling for the phantom camera all the way back to Three building, and what happened there was like something out of the movies too. Larry Gaines overtook him on the stairs, turned back, gave him an unforgettable smile and said "Nice going, Gypsy."

Chapter 3

The Dorset *Chronicle* was held in low esteem among extracurricular activities. Being a member of its staff might look good on your record, and in the yearbook, but that seemed scarcely worth the amount of work it took.

The editor-in-chief was usually a sixth-former, heavy with other honors, who delegated most of the responsibility to his managing editor. And when the managing editor was someone like John Haskell, a glutton for punishment and a stern taskmaster, it was only common sense to stay away from the whole enterprise. The paper was always understaffed — Haskell sometimes claimed to have written every word of it

himself — but it came out faithfully every two weeks, in
press runs of a thousand copies or more.

Knoedler called it "one of our best public-relations tools,"
and you could see what he meant. There wasn't much to
admire in the way the *Chronicle* was written or edited, but
it looked good: handsomely printed on slick paper in four- or
six- or eight-page issues, four columns to the page, with a
liberal use of photographs. Anyone picking it up and looking
it over would have had to assume that a good deal of money
had gone into its making. And only rarely did messages like
"With the Compliments of a Friend" or "Buy War Bonds"
appear in its advertising space; most of the ads were display
items from reputable merchants in Hartford and Boston and
New York who must have considered Dorset a "real" enough
school to warrant their business. The paper had the aspect
of something settled and solvent — and that, for a school in
financial trouble, amounted to good public relations indeed.

On deadline afternoons, and usually in the very nick of
time, John Haskell would stack up the messy copy and pictures and send them off to a commercial printing plant in
Meriden; a few days later heavy packages of freshly cast
linotype and photo-engravings would arrive back at the
school, and then it was time to put the thing together.

The craft of printing had been one of Mrs. Hooper's minor
enthusiasms, so there was a well-equipped, picturesque little
printshop tucked into the campus. A pale, sour man named
Mr. Gold was in charge there, possibly the only communist
on the Dorset payroll, doing his quiet best to keep the kids
from driving him crazy as he went about what he always
called "the job." Much of his time was spent in preparing
sumptuous school catalogues and sleek little promotional
brochures (Knoedler ordered more brochures than any of the
three other headmasters in Mr. Gold's memory), and the

coming of each spring brought additional workloads in the yearbook pages and the Commencement Day programs; but at bi-weekly intervals, all through the year, everything in the shop had to be set aside for the *Chronicle*.

Haskell considered it part of a managing editor's duty to be on hand when the paper went to press. He would stride around the printshop trailing a handful of galley proofs, pausing to peer over the shoulders of boys who stood working on page forms at the composing table or hand-setting type for the larger headlines. Only one or two of them were members of the *Chronicle* staff; the others, mostly younger, were kids who'd drawn the printshop as their community-service assignment. Their talk bristled with terms of the printing trade — "stick," "quoine," "slug," "furniture," "carding-out" — as if in an effort to convince themselves they were really journeymen printers and not schoolboys at all.

"Hey, I need more furniture," one of them said one afternoon.

"Need more what?" Haskell inquired.

"Furniture."

"What's that?"

And wholly unaware that he was being kidded, speaking as patiently as if Haskell were an apprentice in the shop, the boy explained what "furniture" was, while Haskell listened and nodded with a straight face. Afterwards, Haskell ventured a conspiratorial wink at Mr. Gold, who had heard it all, and Mr. Gold allowed himself a qualified smile as he bent over his own part of the job again.

Mr. Gold despised all Dorset boys on principle — rich, spoiled little snot-noses — but he had to admit that this particular fellow, this Haskell, was kind of an interesting kid. He was smart, witty, and very well-read for his age; last fall the two of them had hung around the shop for half an hour after quitting time one day, talking politics, and Haskell had displayed a surprisingly sound grasp of Marxist theory. But when Mr. Gold tried to tell his wife about it that night, in the kitchen of their home in Unionville, she didn't want to listen. " 'Interesting'?" she repeated. "You're telling me 'interesting' and 'sophisticated' about some fifteen-year-old *prep* school kid? Come on. I think you're going soft in the head, Sidney." And he guessed she was right; he had probably been taken in. Besides, there were unattractive things about Haskell too: the supercilious manner, the theatrical way he talked and moved around.

If Haskell could be theatrical in the printshop, he was worse in the *Chronicle* office. And he spent as much time as he could in the office, far more time than was necessary.

"And do you realize?" he demanded of Hugh Britt one evening, pacing the floor for emphasis, "Do you realize I've written the last four editorials for him? *And* made up the staff assignments. *And* edited all the copy, not to mention writing most of it. He sits up there wrapping friction tape around his hockey stick, or rubbing neat's-foot oil into his baseball glove, and saying he's too busy. Too busy. Well, it's got to stop, that's all. It's got to stop."

"Why don't you lay it on the line with him, John?" Hugh Britt said. "Tell him if you're going to do the editor's work you want to *be* the editor."

Haskell hadn't expected such a clear-cut suggestion. After a moment, smiling vaguely as he paced, he said "Ah, yes, Hughie; if only it were that simple."

The office was in an upstairs section of Four building, well away from the kitchen help's quarters, and it looked as much like a real newspaper office as Haskell could make it. There were two paper-strewn typewriter desks, and there was a hotplate and a coffee percolator with several chipped mugs.

Haskell drank more coffee than he wanted, especially on deadline days; often, when the door was locked and the windows open, he and Britt smoked cigarettes here too.

Haskell took up a slumped, staring posture at the windows, his homely features set in the look of someone for whom one crisis is never enough. "And on top of everything else," he said, "we now have *Grove* to contend with."

"I don't know why you say 'contend,' John."

"Because he'll be around our necks, that's why. We'll be contending with his funny face and his dirty clothes and his awful fingernails, and we'll spend all our time just keeping him *down*. He was up here sucking around and sucking around all afternoon."

"You're making too much of it," Britt said, shifting uncomfortably in his chair. Haskell was his best friend, but there were times when he got on his nerves. Tonight Haskell had brought him up here after study hall, apparently for no other purpose than to dramatize himself. Another thing: Britt wished Haskell would quit calling him "Hughie."

"Shall I put some coffee on?" Haskell inquired.

"No, thanks; I want to get on back."

"What for? There's plenty of time."

"I want to get on back, that's all." And Britt stood up. "John?" he said. "You coming or staying?"

"My goodness," Haskell said, "how abrupt we are this evening."

They didn't talk on their way back to Three building, and it wasn't a companionable silence. Britt walked with a hard ringing of his heels on the flagstones, holding his big shoulders square and tight, wondering how he could possibly admire anyone who said things like "My goodness, how abrupt we are this evening."

They knew something was up as soon as they'd reached

the second floor, and they could sense it was something bad.
Both ends of the hall were unnaturally quiet. Boys stood in
clusters, near and far, their mouths partly open, and they
were all staring at the closed door of Henry Weaver's room.
Ordinarily, nobody paid much attention to Henry Weaver; it
wouldn't have been hard to forget he existed. He was big and
muscular and mild, a good soccer player, a pleasant, smiling
fellow who had no friends.

"Weaver's got a little kid in there with him," somebody
said. "Little kid from Two building."

Then Pete Giroux went up with a bar of soap in his hand
and wrote "HOMO" across Weaver's door. All the dormitory
doors were made of dark wood, finely and deeply grooved; it
would be impossible to wash the lettering out of those
grooves. A plainly legible ghost of it would be there next
year, when somebody else moved into the room; it would be
there forever, unless workmen came and replaced the door.

"Come on outa there, Weaver," Pete Giroux called like a
cop in the movies, "or we're coming inta get ya." Another
boy was crouched and working with a jackknife at the
wooden bolt of the door.

It opened suddenly and very briefly, just enough to let the
little kid out into the hall. He stood there blinking in his
rumpled dinner clothes, trying to look as if he didn't know
what this was all about. He was twelve or thirteen. Haskell,
who knew the names and faces of everyone in school from his
work on the *Chronicle,* identified him as Dwight Reeves of
the first form.

"Arright," Giroux told him, "getcher ass outa here, punk.
Fast."

Then they concentrated on "getting" Henry Weaver,
though there was no clear plan for what to do when they got
him. The jackknife couldn't pick the bolt open when

Weaver's hands were holding it shut, so they fell back on other tactics. Somebody came from the shower room with a water-filled condom and shoved the bulging, wobbling thing over the transom into Weaver's room, where it fell and burst with a heavy splash. Soon a chant went up from the crowd, quietly at first and then louder: "Ho-mo; ho-mo; ho-mo . . ."

Weaver was evidently trying to outlast them, to stick it out until Lights, when they'd all have to disperse, and he might have made it except that Steve MacKenzie came strolling lazily into the hall and said "What the hell's going on?" When he'd heard the news he went up very close to Weaver's door and said "Weaver? I guess you know that if I report this you'll be expelled tomorrow. Now. I want you to come on out of there."

And Weaver came out. He looked terrible, and the worst part was that he was smiling.

Pete Giroux took the scruff of his neck in one hand and the seat of his pants in the other; they frog-marched him down to the shower room, pushed him fully dressed into a cold shower and held him there for a long time. He smiled under the water, too, and all the way back to his room, where he closed and bolted his door again.

"And so ends another night of fun and frolic in the dorm," Haskell said to Britt, who wasn't listening.

Two new boys had come to the second floor of Three building in January, and by now it was clear how they were turning out. One of them, Jim Pomeroy, was small and trim and athletic, so it had been assumed at once that he'd be a neat companion for Terry Flynn. Pomeroy was in the fourth form, as befitted his age, but apart from that he and Flynn seemed to have everything in common. They even looked something alike, except that Flynn was blond and Pomeroy dark. Pomeroy had muscle definition too. On spring afternoons they would jog and sprint around the big lawn in front of One building until dusk, expertly and gracefully passing a football back and forth, two peppy little Irish-American guys without a care in the world. It soon developed too that Pomeroy was "sophisticated" — he knew a lot about girls and could talk about them without seeming to boast. This might tend to make some of his listeners withdraw in an envious, embarrassed silence after a while, but it went over very well with others, and especially with Steve MacKenzie: there was nothing MacKenzie liked better than talking about girls. Almost every night, after Lights and after Mr. Driscoll's rounds, he and several others would drop into Pomeroy's or Flynn's room, and the sounds of their murmuring and lewd laughter would float down the hall for hours.

The other new boy was tall and slim with a strikingly handsome face, a bad complexion, and the unfortunate name of Pierre Van Loon. From the very beginning he'd made the mistake of talking too much, and the further mistake of talking about boring things: he would tell in painstaking detail the plots of rocket-ship stories from *Astounding Science Fiction* magazine, or relate with wonderment his father's adventures as an artillery officer in the First World War. At other times he could be found in one of the toilet stalls with his pants around his ankles, sitting much longer than necessary in the smell of his own excrement and wholly absorbed in a comic-book.

Pierre Van Loon tried hanging around with Lear and Jennings for a while until they grew impatient with him, then he drifted down among the less popular; he might even have tried Henry Weaver, except that he'd been present on the night of Weaver's humiliation. Eventually he settled on Grove.

"I'm doing a little better, don't you think?" he said in Grove's room one afternoon. "I mean I still do dumb things and everything, but I don't do anything quite as dumb as when I first got here."

"Well," Grove said kindly, "it takes a little time."

"Like, did I tell you about the first time I met Mr. Draper? I'd only been here about a week, and I don't take chemistry, you see, that's the thing. If I took chemistry, I'd have known him. Anyway, he came walking toward me in the whaddya-callit, the quadrangle, and he was sort of smiling at me — that's the thing; if he hadn't been smiling I wouldn't have said it — so I smiled right back and I said 'What's the matter, sir, got a stone in your shoe?' "

"Oh. So what did he say?"

"Oh, he was very nice about it; he just said 'No, I've had polio.' And then of course I spent about half an hour apologizing, and he kept saying it was all right, but still. Boy. Wow. Jesus."

"Well, those things happen."

"What've you got there, Grove? Is that English or history?"

"Just something for the *Chronicle.*"

"Oh, yeah? You really put in a lot of work on that, don't you. Know something? That's something I'd like to do too."

"Well, you'd have to wait till next year now; then you could sign up for it."

"I see. Well, I wouldn't want to do the serious stuff or anything, but I could do the funny stuff. You going someplace?"

"Just to take this over to Haskell."

"Mind if I come along?"

"Well," Grove said, "the thing is I have to talk to Haskell about this, you see." And he got out of there fast, before Van Loon could say anything else. Even for a chronic loser like William Grove, some guys were a little hard to take.

The door of the *Chronicle* office was locked; he had to knock and announce his name before being allowed inside, where Haskell and Britt were smoking cigarettes.

"Well, Willie Grove," Haskell said. "What've you brought us this time?" He took Grove's manuscript and dropped it on the desk after a cursory glance; then he went on pacing the floor. He was wearing his suit coat like a cloak, the empty sleeves dangling. "Sit down, Grove," he said. "We're in a mood of celebration today. A sad day in some ways, but essentially a day of brave beginnings. Our leader has stepped aside."

"Oh?" Grove said. "So does that mean you're the editor now?"

"It does indeed. There won't be any formal announcement, of course, but for anyone who's interested the old masthead will carry the news in our very next issue. And our good friend Hughie here is now managing editor. I only hope he enjoys it more than I did."

"Well, that's — good," Grove said. "Congratulations."

"Ah, Willie. I knew I could count on you to say precisely the right thing. Cigarette?"

Grove had smoked two cigarettes in his life, and they'd both made him sick. "No, thanks," he said, and hoped Haskell wouldn't press him.

"I've been meaning to tell you, Grove," Haskell said, "how much we've enjoyed your stories. They've needed scarcely any work at all. Also, I'm delighted that you've cut and cleaned your fingernails. You're almost human now."

"Hey, John?" Britt said. "Where'd you get this phony way

of talking, anyway? All this plum-in-your-mouth stuff? Because I mean it's really getting to be a pain in the ass."

"Is this a faculty meeting, or what?" Myra Stone inquired of her husband as he prepared to leave the house.

"No," he said, "just something I want to see Knoedler about."

"Can't you even tell me what it is?"

"Well, I think I'd rather not, dear. It's about one of the boys, and you're friendly with a good many of them."

"Oh, Edgar, honestly. You and your secrets. You make me so *tired.*"

"You make me tired, too, Myra, but somehow we get along."

She followed him as far as the front door. "Will you be back by five? Because Edith said she'd call at five. Don't you even care about your daughter?"

"All I care about is myself," he said. "Everybody knows that."

"Think you're so funny, don't you. Well, you're not funny at all. You're remote and you're distant and you're cold. You're cold."

When he'd gone she walked the floor for a long time with one hand at her forehead. She might have cried, except that it almost never occurred to her to cry when she was alone.

"Sorry to drop in on you this way, uh, Alcott," Stone said.

"Not at all. A little sherry?"

"No, thanks."

And as he closed the sherry cupboard Knoedler tried to compose a sentence in his mind: If it's a question of money,

Edgar, there's no reason why we can't get together on a
satisfactory . . . The trouble with such a sentence was that
it wouldn't be true. Stone was the highest-paid man on the
staff, and any further raise would break the bank. Still, they
couldn't afford to lose him: he was their only Harvard graduate and one of their only two Ph.D.s.

"It's about one of the boys," Stone began, and Knoedler
felt his lungs loosen in relief. "It's Haskell, in the fourth
form. I think he may be heading for some sort of nervous or
emotional — well, these things aren't easy to assess, but he
shows signs of being disturbed."

"Mm," Knoedler said. "Well, the last time Haskell's name
came up, I remember you described him as brilliant."

"I don't think I said that, Alcott. I think I said precocious.
He's always tended to show off in class — he doesn't just talk,
he holds forth — but lately he's begun holding forth in a very
elevated style, and sometimes I can't make sense of it. And
it's the same in his written work, pages on pages. I tried to
have a talk with him after class today, and I couldn't seem
to hold his attention."

Knoedler was nodding slowly and steadily to show that he
understood. "Well," he said at last, "I know John's been
under pressure from overwork on the school paper, and then
of course he's always been a high-strung boy and something
of an eccentric; there's a rather bizarre family situation, and
so on. In any case — "

"Bizarre in what way?"

"Well, the parents were divorced long ago; the mother's
since been married and divorced two or possibly three more
times; she now lives with a young man who runs a riding
stable over here in Glastonbury. But the point is a good
many of the boys come from troubled homes, Edgar, as I'm

sure you know, and we have to allow a certain leeway in our
— our judgments."

"I didn't mean to be making a judgment, Alcott," Stone
said. "I simply meant — well, for one thing I wanted to ask
if the infirmary has access to a psychiatrist."

"Oh, I expect something of that sort could be arranged if
necessary, yes," Knoedler said, but he was beginning to be
impatient. This, after all, was Edgar Stone's first year here.
New masters often tended to expect a schoolful of frightened
little conformists; it took a while to understand Dorset Academy. "In any case I'm glad you stopped by, Edgar," he said.
"I'll have a talk with him tomorrow."

That evening at dinner, for the first time, William Grove
found himself sitting with Haskell and Britt and being included in their talk. He could scarcely believe it.

". . . Christianity doesn't *begin* to answer the needs of this
century," Haskell said, while Britt nodded in agreement
over a forkful of succotash, and Grove quickly saw an opening.

"That's why we have Marx and Freud, I guess," he said,
not at all sure that it wasn't something he'd read in *Time*
magazine.

"Exactly," Haskell said. "And very well put, Grove. Because if Marx and Freud hadn't existed, we'd have invented
them. What's more, we'd . . ."

That was the only time Haskell said "very well put,
Grove," but the talk went happily on long after they'd left
the refectory, and Grove remained a part of it. The three of
them strolled around the quadrangle until time for study
hall, talking and talking, making occasional sweeping gestures with their arms. Haskell had abandoned Christianity

now and moved down into popular culture. The function of
the movies, he explained, was to help people hide from reality.

"Oh, I don't know," Grove said, because it seemed important to disagree sometimes. "What about a movie like *The
Grapes of Wrath?*"

"That's an evasion of reality too, don't you see? When
everything's tied up in a neat little dramatic package, you
can forget it the minute you walk out of the theater."

"So what do you *want,* John?" Hugh Britt said. "You want
everybody to go out and be migrant workers or Russian
revolutionaries or something?"

"I want people to *feel,*" Haskell told him. "I want people
to experience *life.*"

All the next day, even through his afternoon of jolting
around in the truck, Grove went over and over the talk in
his mind. He had said three or possibly four smart things,
and might have said more except that he'd had the sense to
keep quiet when Haskell went off on one of his long speeches,
or when Haskell and Britt were bickering. There had been
two or three times too when he'd screwed-up and said something dumb, but lapses like that would be easy to correct in
future dinners and strolls.

He was getting dressed for dinner that night when Britt
came to his room and said "Grove? Can I come in? Can I shut
the door?"

And Britt sat on Grove's chair, looking trim and spruce as
he always did in his evening clothes. "Listen," he said. "Haskell's cracking up. I've seen it coming for a long time; maybe
you have too. Anyway, Knoedler called him into the office
today, and when he came out he could hardly wait to tell me
about it. Or I guess he *wanted* to tell me, but I couldn't make
head or tail out of it. All very emotional and overwrought.

He told me he'd said to Knoedler, 'Sir, before you go any further I want you to know that I love this school.' I said 'What'd you say *that* for, John? You don't "love" the school, do you?' And then he told me he cried — sat there crying in front of Old Bottle-ass — and he damn near cried again just telling me about it. I said 'What'd you *cry* for?' And all he gave me was more of this convoluted bullshit. Well, if he's sick, let him go to a hospital. And whether he's sick or not, I've had enough. So listen, Grove: let's steer clear of him tonight, okay? I don't know about you, but I'm fed up with being his psychiatrist, or his mother, or whatever the hell it is he wants me to be."

They couldn't steer clear of him at dinner because he sat down with them, but he was silent throughout the meal. It was a dramatic silence, giving every sign of wanting to call attention to itself. Whenever they glanced at him they found his face set in a haggard look, or in a despairing little smile, and so they tried not to glance at him at all.

It was easy to get away from him when the refectory emptied out: all they had to do was walk fast. They hurried around to Three building, considered going upstairs but decided against it, struck out across the quadrangle and all the way through to the front of One building, and kept on walking. "I just don't want him catching up with us," Britt explained.

A hundred yards up the main driveway they moved out onto the lawn and sat on the grass beneath a clump of trees. From here they could look back on the long front of One building, purple in the blue haze of dusk, and they watched the dark cavity of its archway. Soon Haskell came out, alone, looking very small in the distance, wearing his coat like a cloak, and began slowly pacing right and left.

"He can't see us," Britt said. "We're in shadow here, but he knows we're up here somewhere. Watch him."

They both watched him. Britt plucked a blade of grass and chewed it for a while, then spat it out with more force than necessary. "He's waiting for us to go down to *him*," he said. "Well, let him wait. Let him wait."

"Jean-Paul?" Alice Draper inquired later that night. "If I ask you something, will you promise to tell me the truth?"

"Of course."

She was lying in his bed with the covers thrown back, propped on one elbow so that her small, pretty breasts lolled to one side. La Prade was up and rummaging in his desk for cigarettes.

"Do you still find me attractive?"

"What a foolish question," he said. Then he straightened up from the desk and turned to face her with a smile intended to be both reassuring and devilish. "You ought to know better than that, Alice." And that was certainly true: if he didn't still find her attractive, why had he failed to break off with her last fall?

"Well," she said, "I know you like to have sex with me" (and "to have sex with" had always struck him as one of the more barbarous of American idioms, but he let it pass); "it's just that I don't think you'd really care very much if I stopped coming over here. You'd just have one of the infirmary nurses, or something."

"Both the infirmary nurses are lesbians and they have each other," he said. "I thought everybody knew that."

"Oh, that's nonsense. The younger one has Paul what's-his-name, the art teacher. I thought everybody knew *that.* Anyway, the point is — "

"The point is you want me to tell you I love you," he said,

moving toward the bed. "Well, that's easy. I love you." And
for the moment at least, it was easy indeed. He was looking
at her long thighs, one partly covering the other, and at her
knees. Some women's knees had bulky caps, others had thick
crescents of gristle on the insides, but Alice Draper's were
perfect. They were narrow, precise little skull-shaped forma-
tions, faintly blue- or yellow-tinted according to their degree
of flexion; they looked delicious.

He was moving his lips and tongue around one of them
now, while the other shyly waited for attention at his cheek;
then his mouth went on up the inside of one warm thigh,
which came apart from the other and opened for him.

". . . What's *that?*" she cried, going suddenly stiff.

"What's what?"

"That light — there was a streak of *light* across the wall."

"Oh, it's only Bob Driscoll with his silly flashlight; you
know he goes past here every night."

"Well, but it wasn't just going past; it was like someone
trying to look *in.*"

"Don't be silly, Alice. Nobody could see through these curtains."

"Are you sure?"

"Of course I'm sure. Will you please try to relax?"

Alone on the second-floor landing of Three building, Steve
MacKenzie stood slumped and waiting with his fingers in his
hip pockets. His big face looked righteous; when the waver-
ing beam of Driscoll's flashlight came up the stairwell, he
was ready for it.

"Sir, Haskell's not here," he reported.

"Oh?" Driscoll said. "Any idea where he is?"

"No, sir. I saw him in study hall, but not since then."

And when Driscoll had gone, MacKenzie felt a pleasant sense of having done the right thing. If it had been Terry Flynn or Jim Pomeroy, or even Lear or Jennings, he would have covered for them: those guys would only have been up to some devilment, and could always be counted on to look out for him as well as for themselves. But where was the percentage in sticking your neck out for a creep like Haskell?

". . . And you did say to keep an eye on him, Alcott," Robert Driscoll said in Knoedler's living room, "so I thought you'd want to know about this. I've looked everywhere."

Knoedler, roused from bed and wearing a surprisingly cheap-looking bathrobe and pajamas, rubbed his face. "I knew I shouldn't have let him leave the office alone today," he said. "I should've taken him over to the infirmary, if nothing else. Well, what now? Should we call the family first, or the police?"

"Police first, I guess," Driscoll said.

"No, wait, Bob. He's probably only trying to get home. Glastonbury isn't far. Let's start over there, and I imagine we'll find him walking along the road. Give me five minutes to get dressed."

And they set out, in Knoedler's car, on a white Connecticut highway under a full moon. Dense black masses of trees sped away on either side of their headlights; there were no other cars on the road. Driscoll rode in silence. He was reasonably sure that in a real school there wouldn't be situations like this.

"Well, it's only three or four more miles," Knoedler said at the wheel. "This is very — distressing."

And then the headlights picked him out — a small figure

trudging along the right-hand side of the road, wearing what looked like a short cloak, turning, as the car approached, to raise one thumb in a hitchhiker's appeal.

Knoedler brought the car to a stop and switched on the ceiling light to let Haskell see who they were.

"Oh, my God, Mr. Knoedler," he said. "Mr. Driscoll. This is — God, I — " His eyes were round, and there were black ridges of dust-caked spit on his lips. He had removed his stiff collar and tie, but the tiny knob of his gold collar-button gleamed in the moonlight; any cop for miles around would have spotted him as a Dorset boy.

"Get in, John," Knoedler said. "All we want to do is take you home."

"Sir, I'm not going back to school, and that's final. That's final."

"I didn't mean school, John, I meant home. That's probably best now, don't you think?"

"Ah." Haskell took three steps backward onto the shoulder of the road and stood glaring at them, giving a little toss of his head to show how ludicrous all this was. "Ah. So now I've been expelled."

Driscoll sighed and said "Oh, Lord." Then he got out of the car, leaving the door open, and climbed into the back seat. "Come on, Haskell," he said. "Let's quit fooling around. You ride up front."

It took a few more minutes of trying to reason with him, but he came along. They made another stop at a telephone booth where Knoedler called Haskell's mother, remembering just in time that she preferred to be called Mrs. Atwood, the name of her second or third husband; then they found their way to a modest white house among many trees.

They were greeted by a man of twenty-eight or thirty, handsome enough to be a romantic actor, whose name was lost in the mumbled introductions and who looked a little lost himself as he ushered them into the living room. "Mrs. Atwood'll be right down," he said. "Can I get you something?"

"Oh, no, thanks," Knoedler said, settling himself in an upholstered chair.

Driscoll, who had chosen a straight chair as if to prove his readiness to leave at any moment, was looking around the room in mild surprise: he would have thought most Dorset boys came from wealthier homes than this.

"Well," the young man said to Haskell. "How're you doin', buddy?" And he looked embarrassed as soon as he'd said it, even before Haskell fixed him with a wan little smile of disdain. It was clear that "How're you doin', buddy?" was the young man's standard salutation for this strange, homely boy, this sixteen-year-old intellectual who could never be wholly relied on to stay out of sight.

"As far as you're concerned," Haskell told him carefully, giving full weight to each word, "I'm fine."

The young man strolled over to the foot of the stairs, as if that might bring Mrs. Atwood down sooner. He was graceful in his uneasiness, standing with his thumbs in the pockets of his Western jeans, studying the carpet.

When she did come down, Driscoll couldn't take his eyes off her. She wasn't exactly pretty — there was too much of Haskell in her face for that — but she was as regal as the leading actress in some Broadway play of which he'd seen only still photographs, and she seemed to smolder as she walked.

She went first to her son and told him he looked "dreadful"; then she turned to the young man and said "Evan, why don't you and John go out on the porch, so I can talk to these gentlemen alone."

It seemed to be the last thing either of them wanted to do, but they went; apparently she was accustomed to having her way.

"Could we start at the beginning, please, Mr. Knoedler?" she said, and she seated herself in a way that emphasized the swing and rustle of her full skirt. "Can you tell me what's been going on in that romantic-looking little school of yours?"

Knoedler cleared his throat. "Well, John's been under a good deal of pressure lately, Mrs. Atwood," he began, "and he's always been a high-strung boy, as you know. I'm not a physician, but I understand that sometimes the nerves reach a kind of crisis point, and then it's advisable to seek therapeutic help . . ."

The talk went on for perhaps another twenty minutes, and Driscoll contributed nothing to it. This was Knoedler's baby; let Knoedler handle it. Besides, it was too late at night for being helpful in anything, let alone in something he didn't understand. He wanted to go home and sleep.

Then suddenly Mrs. Atwood got up, piqued by something Knoedler had said — something Driscoll hadn't even caught — and walked away to the mantelpiece, where she whirled to face him again.

"It strikes me, Mr. Knoedler," she said, "that you people run a pretty funny school. What do you *do* to the kids there? What do they do to each other? I send you a great deal of money to prepare my son for college and he comes home looking crucified, and all you can do is sit around making little innuendos about my private life."

"I was aware of no innuendos, Mrs. Atwood," Knoedler said, blushing. "I certainly meant nothing of the sort, and I — "

"Oh, come off it, Knoedler." She snatched up a cigarette

and lighted it swiftly; then she started talking again with the cigarette wagging in her lips. "You're *dying* to know about Evan. Well, apart from the fact that it's none of your business — " She tore the cigarette from her mouth — "Evan is the finest riding instructor in this part of the state. He and I are partners in what happens to be an excellent stable, and I imagine we bring a great deal more care and professionalism to our work than you do to yours."

They were all on their feet now. "Mrs. Atwood," Knoedler said. "I hope you'll understand that I — "

"Thank you for bringing my son home," she said, "and beyond that, thank you for nothing. Thank you for nothing at all."

When she switched on the porch light for them it disclosed Evan seated alone at one end of the long porch and Haskell at the other. Neither of them got up to say goodnight.

In the car going back to school Knoedler said "I don't see what more we could have done."

"No," Driscoll said.

They were both silent for a few miles, until Knoedler started to talk in a rambling way about "values."

". . . and the family structure as you and I know it is rapidly disappearing, Bob," he was saying. "If the school stays in business I imagine we'll see more and more evidence of that in the next few years."

"Yeah," Driscoll said; and at least two more miles went by before he said "Alcott?"

"Mm?"

"How do you mean, 'if the school stays in business'?"

Chapter

There was a rule at Dorset that you had to room alone during your first year; having a roommate was a privilege reserved for "old" boys. This made for a good deal of emotional tension every May, when the double-room assignments were given out.

"Hey," one boy would say shyly to another. "Want to get a room together next year?"

"Well, the thing is I've already promised somebody else."

"Oh."

For a week the quadrangle pulsed with awkward little conversations like that; it was a time of subtle pursuit and hurt feelings and last-minute settlings for second best.

Terry Flynn and Jim Pomeroy formed a happy exception
— everybody knew they were made for each other — and
there were other logical pairings such as Lear and Jennings.

Britt and Haskell would have been naturals too, but Haskell was gone — and this filled William Grove with a terrible
mixture of doubt and hope. He knew he had almost no
chance with somebody like Hugh Britt; still, Britt did tolerate him in ways that showed every sign of turning into lik-
ing. And they had spent a great amount of time together
lately, if only in preparing the *Chronicle*'s eight-page Commencement Issue.

"Hey, Grove," Britt said in the office one afternoon, "I
don't like this headline of yours, ' "Smudge" Parker Dies
Hero's Death.' "

"Well, but he did, though," Grove said. "The point is, he
could've bailed out, but he stayed in his plane and steered it
away from this English village; that's why they gave him
the — "

"I know, I know," Britt said impatiently, "but the headline
doesn't have any dignity. The story doesn't either, for that
matter — all this gee-whiz, boy's-magazine stuff. It's vulgar.
It's tawdry. Don't you see? Look. Make it something like this:
'James Parker Killed in England.' Then your lead ought to
be: 'James H. Parker, class of '39, was killed after steering
his crippled fighter plane away from the English village of
Whaddyacallit last month,' period. 'He was posthumously
awarded the Distinguished Service Cross,' period.

"New paragraph: 'A first lieutenant with the such-and-
such Fighter Command of the something Air Force, Parker
had served so-and-so many months overseas,' and so on.
Then you can save your 'Smudge' business for the third or
fourth paragraph: 'Parker, known affectionately as
"Smudge" to his Dorset friends,' and et cetera. See?"

"Oh," Grove said. "I guess so, yeah. Okay, I'll do it over."
Britt seemed always to be right in matters where vulgarity
and tawdriness were concerned.

They worked in silence for an hour or so, long after Britt
had approved Grove's second version of the Smudge Parker
story; then Britt said "Hey, Grove?"

"Yeah?"

"Listen. I've been thinking. I don't really want to be editor
of this thing next year. It takes up too much time, and I can't
afford to let my grades slip. I wouldn't mind helping out here,
but I don't want the responsibility. How about you doing it?"

Grove was astonished. "Editor-in-*chief,* you mean?"

"Oh, come on. It's only a dumb little school paper. You can
handle it."

Nobody had ever before expressed confidence in Grove's
ability to handle anything. "Well," he said, "I guess I could
give it a try."

"Okay. Let's set it up that way, then. You be editor and I'll
be managing editor — or maybe we could call it 'associate
editor'; that suggests less authority. I think it'll work out.
And I mean hell, we certainly aren't going to find anyone
else to do it." Britt had finished his share of the day's work.
He got up, put on his Dorset blazer and pulled it straight as
he made for the door.

"Hey, Britt?" Grove said. "You got a roommate for next
year?"

Britt hesitated. "Well, Ed Kimball's asked me," he said. "I
guess I'll probably go in with him."

"Oh." Ed Kimball was a hunched, plump fellow, a wizard
at math and chemistry; all he and Britt had in common was
that they were both straight-A students.

With his hand on the knob of the open door, Britt seemed
to be thinking it over. "I don't know, Grove," he said. "I can

see where it might be all right to room with you; I've considered it — we have a lot in common and all that — but I don't know. There's something a little too undisciplined about you. For me, anyway."

"How do you mean?"

"Oh, you know. You're always late for everything; you flunk courses and don't seem to care; you're sloppy; that kind of thing could make trouble if we roomed together. Besides, you're — well, you've come a long way this year, that's true, but last fall I thought you were — unwholesome, sort of."

Grove's mouth went dry. "How do you mean, 'unwholesome'?"

"Oh, come on, Grove. You know. I was there the night those guys ganged you and jerked you off."

"They *didn't* jerk me off! They couldn't even get me to — "

"What the hell's the difference? If it'd been me I'd have killed them. I'd have killed the first son of a bitch that touched me."

"How? Whaddya gonna do when eight guys are holding you down?"

"I don't want to talk about it," Britt said. "All I know is you were lying there laughing and talking away; you might as well've been saying 'Do it more.' "

"I *wasn't*. I was trying to make a *joke* of it. Can't you see that?"

"No," Britt said. "No, I'm sorry, but I can't see that at all." There was a silence while they looked briefly at each other and then at the floor. At last Britt said "Well, hell, let's forget it. I'm sorry I brought it up. Look, I'm going on back to the dorm. You coming?"

"No, I want to finish this stuff," Grove said. But he didn't finish anything. All he did was stare at the papers on the desk, turning over the word "unwholesome" in his mind. After a long time he closed up the office and went back to Three building.

Pierre Van Loon wasn't in his room, and the toilet stalls were vacant too, but Grove found him fooling around to no apparent purpose in the dim storage alcove where trunks and suitcases were kept. "Hey, Van Loon?" he said.

"Yeah?"

"Want to get a room together next year?"

During that summer the parents of all Dorset students received a form letter from W. Alcott Knoedler announcing that dress would be optional in the coming year.

William Grove came back to school with two new suits, blue and brown, both purchased by his father at Bond's in Times Square. He thought they were fine until he began to notice that almost nobody else wore clothes like that: most people didn't wear suits at all, but tweed jackets with gray flannel pants. Their coats had practically no shoulder padding and their pants had no pleats (he remembered now having noticed that in the old school uniforms, too). Looking around, he could count only three boys who dressed the way he did: Albert Canzoneri, whose father was the shop teacher; Lothar Brundels, whose father was the chef; and Gus Gerhardt, whose father was the groundskeeper at Miss Blair's, a famous girls' school twelve miles away.

Grove couldn't be bothered with Canzoneri, and he was afraid of Gerhardt — almost everybody was afraid of Gerhardt — but Lothar Brundels took over the humor column of the *Chronicle* that September, so there was an opportunity to discuss clothes with him in the office one day.

"Whaddya mean, 'proletarian'?" Brundels said. "You're a

funny kid, Grove. *Sure* we look 'proletarian.' Why the hell shouldn't we? Listen. You know every Thanksgiving? When all the parents come for the big-assed turkey dinner? And afterwards old Knoedler rings his bell and makes this corny speech about how very, very much we owe the chef, and then he calls 'Come on out here, Louie, we want to thank you' — and everybody claps, and this funny little guy 'Louie' comes bouncing out of the kitchen waving his arms over his head, all smiles, all in white, with this big chef's hat and this napkin tied around his neck, and son of a bitch, Grove, that's my father. How the fuck do you *think* it makes me feel?"

Grove's own father came up from New York for a visit later in the fall, and he looked surprisingly short when Grove met him outside the One building archway.

"Well," the elder Grove said as they started through the quadrangle, "this certainly is an impressive place."

"Yeah, well, it's very well designed. It's called 'Cotswold' architecture."

"So how're you doing, Bill? Staying out of trouble?"

"I guess so."

"You certainly are tall."

"Yeah."

"How's the math coming? Think you might pass math this time?"

"I don't know. Hope so."

"Well, you know, with a thing like math it's mostly a question of mental attitude."

"I know; I know."

For reasons he would never understand, Grove found it all but impossible to call his father "Dad." He remembered having no trouble with the more childish "Daddy," years ago, but "Dad" eluded his tongue. He tried to avoid the problem, on the rare occasions when he saw the man, by arranging his remarks in such a way as to require calling him nothing at all.

In a sidelong look, he tried to assess his father's clothes. There was nothing "proletarian" about his dark, three-piece business suit, though it did look a little shiny from wear, but it was decidedly middle-class. Across the vest hung a delicate gold watch chain that trembled as he walked. Grove was fairly sure most men had wristwatches nowadays, but his father probably hadn't noticed the changing fashion, or didn't care. He wore a pearl-gray fedora with the suit, and highly polished black shoes that looked very small and narrow on the flagstones.

"Good lord," he said, "it must have cost a fortune to build this place."

"Well, I guess it did. There's a crazy old lady named Mrs. Hooper who built it; she probably used up all her husband's money on it. I think he was in steel, or something."

" 'In steel'? How do you mean, 'in steel'?"

"I don't know; he was real rich, that's all I know, and I guess she had money of her own too."

"How do you mean she's crazy?"

"I don't know; it's just what I've heard. She's supposed to be very eccentric and everything."

When they'd walked enough for his father to see most of the architecture, Grove took him up to the *Chronicle* office — it was all he had to be proud of — and showed him that.

"I think it's fine that you've done so well on the paper," his father said, looking uncomfortable in one of the office chairs. "And it's an interesting paper; I enjoy reading it. Still, I wonder if you're not giving it too much of your time."

"Yeah, well, the thing is I enjoy it."

"I know you do. But don't they have a rule here that you can't take part in extracurricular activities unless you keep your grades up?"

"No, there's no rule like that." And Grove risked a small, cynical smile that he was aware of having copied from Haskell. "It's a pretty funny school," he said.

"A funny school?"

"Well, I mean — *you* know — they sort of encourage the extracurricular stuff whether you're a good student or not. They believe in individuality here."

"I see," his father said. "Well, I believe in individuality too, Bill, but I'm not sure how I feel about failing grades in math and failing grades in chemistry and failing grades in French."

This was a jolt: Grove had assumed that his report cards were sent only to his mother, who viewed all such failures as signs of a soul as artistic as her own.

"Why do you suppose you have this trouble with math, Bill?" his father said. "You know something? There are only ten numbers in the world, based on the ten fingers of your hands. The whole science of mathematics follows from that."

"Yeah."

"I think it's mostly a question of mental attitude, don't you? You think it's going to be difficult, so it *is* difficult. You think 'I can't do this,' and then you can't."

"I guess so, yeah," Grove said, and for the first time that afternoon he noticed that his father's face was deeply lined under the eyes and gray with fatigue.

"If you can lick that attitude, Bill, you'll lick the course. You'll be surprised how easy it is. And the same goes for chemistry, because that's mostly just numberwork too. As for the French — well, the French is another matter. There was quite a long note from Mr. — Le Grande?"

"La Prade."

"Right. There was quite a long note from him with your last report card. He feels you have psychological problems."

Grove looked down. "Mental attitude" might be an accept-
able term, but any word beginning with "psych" had come
to frighten him. All such words spoke of a darkness beyond
hope. They reminded him of Haskell. And the worst thing
about them, according to what little he'd been able to read
of Sigmund Freud, was that they had their roots in sexual
anxiety.

"Well," he said, "I don't agree with that. I don't think I
have any psychological problems or anything; French is
hard for me, that's all. I'll try to do better at it, that's all."

And soon he managed to turn the conversation back to the
Chronicle. He gave his father an advance copy of the next
issue, still warm from the press, and pointed out his major
contributions to it — the solemn editorial, a humorous feature on the commando course, the Football Roundup on the
sports page.

"Good," his father said, putting the folded paper away in
his inside pocket. "This'll give me something to read on the
train."

Then they were out in the quadrangle again, and they had
almost reached One building when Steve MacKenzie approached them on the stone walk. Grove hoped MacKenzie
might settle for a nod in passing, but MacKenzie had other
ideas.

"Hi, uh, Bill," he said. "This your dad?" And for three or
four minutes he stood chatting with Grove's father, while
Grove shifted his weight from one foot to the other. At last
MacKenzie held out his hand — it seemed to Grove that
they'd shaken hands at least three times — and said "Well,
I won't keep you, Mr. Grove. Good to meet you, sir."

"There's a nice boy," Mr. Grove said as they walked away.
"He a good friend of yours?"

Out in front of One building, waiting for the taxi, Grove

composed a final sentence in his mind and resolved to deliver
it without stammering. He even rehearsed it, twice, just
under his breath. When the cab pulled up he took his father's hand in a grip that he hoped was as strong as MacKenzie's and said "Thanks for coming out, Dad." It sounded
almost as natural as he'd meant it to.

Terry Flynn and Jim Pomeroy had gotten off to an uneasy
start as roommates on the very first day of school, when
Terry opened a suitcase, said "Look what *I've* got," and
pulled out a set of yellow curtains, pleated and flounced, that
his mother had made especially for their windows.

"Well, that's — nice, Terry," Jim Pomeroy said.

"They're easy to put up," Terry assured him. "I've got the
curtain rods, and the brackets and stuff." And that wasn't
all: he also had eight framed color photographs of rural New
England — from spring wildflowers to autumn foliage to
deep snow — that his mother had thought might brighten
their walls. And he had another photograph, in a stand-up
leather frame to be placed on his side of the windowsill,
showing his mother and father on their wedding day.

"Yeah, well, that's — nice," Jim Pomeroy said. But he
worried about the decorations all day, especially the curtains, until one of the more popular members of his class
dropped in that night and said "Wow, you guys've really
fixed your place up. Looks terrific."

Other visitors soon confirmed that view, and Pomeroy was
able to relax. Still, from time to time, he couldn't help wish-
ing the curtains weren't quite so flouncy, or that there could
be perhaps four — or six, tops — rather than eight of the
framed New England scenes. It was a very small room. He

wished too that Terry Flynn wasn't two years behind him in school.

Football season made everything all right. He and Terry were both Eagles, which everybody said was too bad for the Beavers, and they made an unbeatable combination that year. Because they were both so light (and probably too because they weren't seniors) the Eagles' coach didn't use them for the whole of any game, but when they were in they were tremendous. Pomeroy would fade back, wait for the last possible moment, then leap and throw a long, perfectly spiralling pass, and far down the field the sprinting Flynn always knew just when to turn, reach up, and pick it out of the air.

Grove, who covered the games for the *Chronicle*, soon found he was running out of adjectives for Pomeroy and Flynn, and so as the season wore on his accounts for the sports page lost some of their exuberance. But he enjoyed the work. He himself, on other afternoons, was an absurdly incompetent end on what was called the "intermediate" Beavers' team, but being well known as a non-athlete seemed only to enhance his role as sportswriter. He would shamble along the sidelines, carrying a clipboard and a chewed pencil to record each play; when a game was stalled he would squat and write, holding the clipboard on one tense thigh and very much aware that a number of smaller kids were peering over his shoulder; when the game broke open again he'd get up and run with it, almost as fast as the ball carrier, with the little kids racing in his wake.

His stories usually managed to mention the excellent tackling and blocking of Hugh Britt, who was a sturdy member of the Beavers' line. Even when Britt did nothing distinguished in a game, there would be a sentence near the end about how "sturdy" he had been. Then one afternoon a tangled heap of Eagles and Beavers sorted themselves out, got to their feet and disclosed Hugh Britt lying alone on the grass, face down.

Choppy Tyler blew his whistle and came running, natty and muscle-bound in his referee's uniform of black-striped shirt and white knee pants with black stockings. Miss Logan, the younger and prettier of the two school nurses, walked gravely out onto the field with her hands deep in the pockets of her polo coat. Grove waited until several other people had gathered around Britt; then he tucked the fluttering clipboard under his arm and went out to join them, hoping it might look as though this were part of a journalist's job, but he couldn't see much except the big grass-stained numerals on Britt's jersey.

In the end Britt was carried off the field on a stretcher, to a spatter of applause, and slid into a cream-colored ambulance that took him away to the infirmary. His right leg was broken above the knee.

During the time Britt was laid up, Grove found an easing of pressure in his life. There was no one to admire, no one to please, no one to fear.

He visited Britt in the infirmary once or twice but they couldn't think of much to say, and it was a relief when the visits were over. Most of the time he moved around the campus with a new sense of freedom — and even, occasionally, with a sense of his own importance. There was only one school newspaper, after all, and he was its editor-in-chief. Little kids shyly asked him questions, and boys of his own age and older seemed never to find him ridiculous.

One afternoon there was a knock on the *Chronicle* office door, and he opened it to find a boy named Ward smiling there in a wry but not unfriendly way.

"Mr. Editor," Ward said, "I was just wondering if it's too late to try out for a place on the staff."

"Well, technically, it *is* too late," Grove told him, "but we always need help. I can let you have a couple of assignments. Come on in."

E. Bucknell "Bucky" Ward was one of the new boys in the fifth form that fall, and he had quickly called attention to himself as a campus character. He was pale and sad and looked undernourished; his chest was sunken; he had a deep, hoarse voice and a heavy smoker's cough — that, combined with the nicotine-stained fingers that trembled when he covered his mouth in coughing, provoked most of the laughter that broke around him.

You weren't allowed to smoke at Dorset until you were seventeen, and then only in the Senior Club. Infractions of that rule were punished with many hours of what was called hard labor — not much different from community service, except that it had to be done in addition to the community service requirements. And repeated infractions, as everyone solemnly warned one another, could lead to expulsion from school. But Bucky Ward took reckless chances, nimbly getting away each time, and it wasn't long before he'd earned an outlaw's celebrity. In class, or in assembly, he would sit with a pencil stub the length of a cigarette dangling from his moody lips.

He had been afflicted with many illnesses throughout his childhood, and still enjoyed reciting their medical names in a mock-dramatic voice, but now he was emerging into good health. And whether he looked it or not, he was becoming very strong.

Grove had resented Ward's quick rise to eccentric popularity — it didn't seem fair, in view of his own suffering last year — but he was willing to suspend judgment today. And

he had to acknowledge, as he fingered through the assignment file, that he hadn't really minded Ward's calling him
"Mr. Editor."

"Well," he said, "I suppose somebody ought to cover the
soccer game tomorrow. Think you could do that?"

"Sure," Ward said, "If I can't, I'll fake it."

"Doesn't have to be much; five or six hundred words. Oh,
and I guess we could use a very short feature on Thanksgiving — you know, just some dumb little thing."

"Good," Ward said. "Dumb little things are my favorite
kind."

Within a week they were great companions. Sitting
around the office or strolling the flagstones or taking aimless
walks in the woods, they seemed never to tire of each other's
company. As Grove sometimes reflected, with a touch of
uneasiness, it was almost like falling in love. Bucky Ward
could make him laugh over and over again until he began to
feel like a girl who might at any moment cry "Oh, you keep
me in *stitches!*" What saved him was the nice discovery that
very often, without even seeming to try, he could make
Bucky Ward laugh too.

He was so preoccupied with his new friendship that he
almost missed the deadline for the paper: he and Ward had
to sneak out of their dormitories late one night and meet in
the office, where they fitted "wartime discipline" blackout
panels into the windows, drank dizzying amounts of coffee,
and worked at writing and editing the copy until dawn.

Another night, when they'd sneaked out not to work but
only to fool around the office and talk, Ward fell into one of
his serious moods and told Grove about his girl. Her name
was Polly Clark and she lived in a suburban village adjacent
to Ward's own, just outside of Philadelphia.

"She pretty?" Grove asked.

"I knew you'd ask that. Yes, as it happens, she's pretty, but the point is I wouldn't care if she were plain. I don't suppose you're equipped to understand something like that."

" 'Equipped'? What the hell do you mean, 'equipped'? Jesus, Ward."

"Well, okay; it's just that so many people mistake sex for love."

And Grove had to think that over. "Yeah," he said after a while, "yeah, I guess that's true."

Polly Clark was a wonderful person, Ward explained. She was warm, she was gentle, and he knew he would never find a girl he'd rather marry, when they were old enough, though he guessed there could be no thought of marriage until after the war. And there were other difficulties: "We care very deeply for each other," he said, "but I'm more deeply involved than she is. She says she loves me but she isn't *in* love with me, and when I ask her to clarify that she says she doesn't know her own mind. That hurts. You can't imagine how that hurts."

But Grove thought he could imagine it; at least it seemed so romantic a predicament that he lowered his eyes and felt his own face grow sad and wistful in the look of someone more loving than loved.

"Ah, I don't know," Ward said. "To come so close to all you've ever wanted in life and then never quite — never quite attain it — I suppose that's the nature of the human condition." When Ward was in one of his serious moods, he could seem more serious than anybody else had a right to be.

He had been turning an empty coffee mug around and around in his fingers, staring at it; now in a spasm of revulsion he threw it on the floor, where it bounced and rolled under a chair. He was on his feet and pacing, clawing out his

pack of cigarettes, jabbing one into his mouth and lighting
it savagely as he walked.

"Things!" he said. "Christ, Grove, do you ever get so you
can't stand *things*? *Ob*jects? That cup. This school. Clothes.
Cars. All the God damn senseless *things* in the world. You
oughta see my family's house. Oh, it's very nice and it's very
big and it cost my father a hell of a lot of money, but I can
never make him understand it's just another *thing*. Just
another *thing*. Do you see what I mean at all?"

"Well, sort of," Grove said. "I guess so, yeah." But as Ward
continued to pace and smoke, haggard with tragic vision,
Grove decided he liked him better when he was funny.

Knoedler chimed his table bell after dinner one night, re-
questing silence, and rose to make an announcement. "I
know you'll all join me," he said, "in extending our deepest
sympathy to William Grove, whose father died this morning."

And the people at Grove's table looked around to realize
for the first time that he wasn't there — that he had, in fact,
been gone all day.

Perhaps the only boy in the refectory who had missed him
was Bucky Ward. He'd begun to notice his absence during
school hours, and he'd missed him all afternoon. He had
wondered, with rising jealousy, if Grove might somehow
have arranged to spend the whole day at Hugh Britt's bed-
side in the infirmary — he had even considered going to the
infirmary to find out — but in the end he'd settled for a
brooding, puzzled loneliness. Now Knoedler's announcement made everything clear, and he felt better.

But Steve MacKenzie was shaken by the news. "Oh,

Jesus," he said to Jim Pomeroy. "That's lousy. That's really too bad."

And he was depressed all through study hall that night. He couldn't help pondering how he would feel if his own father were to die. It was unthinkable: Jock MacKenzie was in the very prime of life, a laughing, sailing, golf- and tennis-playing man who could still defeat his son at arm-wrestling any time he felt like it, and often did. Still, there were heart attacks; there were strokes; there was cancer. Nobody lived forever.

Jock MacKenzie's anger could be terrible, but in his gentle moods there was no finer companion in the world. Every worthwhile thing Steve knew, it seemed, was something he had learned from his father. As a condition of receiving a car on his sixteenth birthday, Steve had been made to memorize the whole of Kipling's "If," which later helped him earn the only "A" he'd ever had in Pop Driscoll's course; and certain lines of that poem, remembered now as they sounded in his father's voice, were enough to fill his eyes with tears.

He glanced quickly up and around the study hall, to make sure no one had caught him on the verge of crying; then he pulled himself together and bent over his math assignment. This Sunday, he promised himself, he would call home and have a good long talk with the old man.

When Grove came back to school a few days later, Mac-Kenzie stopped him in the quadrangle and said "Bill, I was really sorry to hear about your dad."

"Yeah, well — thanks."

"Seems like only yesterday he was up here that time," MacKenzie said. "I thought he was a real — a very nice gentleman."

"Yeah. Well, thanks, uh, Steve."

Then MacKenzie noticed that a delicate gold chain hung

from the lapel buttonhole into the breast pocket of Grove's awful blue suit; he almost said "Oh, that's nice; you've got your dad's watch," but decided against it. He had said enough. With one fist he gave Grove a soft cuff on the shoulder; then he walked away.

"When you're talking, Steve," Jock MacKenzie had told him once, "and I don't care who it's to or what it's about, the important thing is knowing when to stop. Never say anything that doesn't improve on silence."

Sometimes the big moves in a man's life, the big changes, announce themselves quickly. Through a journalist friend of his in New York, Jean-Paul La Prade had learned he might qualify for a commission in the O.S.S., and he was eager to pursue it; the difficulty lay in finding a way to tell Alice.

"What does 'O.S.S.' stand for?" she asked him. It was one o'clock in the morning and they were sitting naked on the small sofa in his apartment, drinking bourbon.

"It stands for Office of Strategic Services," he said. "Essentially it's an intelligence operation, very high-level, very secret. There's nothing else like it in the Army. They go in behind enemy lines to gather information, and they report directly to the Chief of Staff. And the point is they need officers who are fluent in French. I could probably be commissioned as a captain."

"Oh, wouldn't that sound nice," she said. " 'Captain La Prade.' " There was an edge of sarcasm in her voice that put him on guard.

"Yes, well, I'm not concerned with how it would sound so much as how it would be. I imagine it might be dangerous. Being dropped in behind enemy lines, not knowing what to expect when you — "

"Ah, you really like saying 'behind enemy lines,' don't you," Alice said. "It makes you feel like something out of the movies, doesn't it. Captain La Prade in Occupied France. Captain La Prade making contact with the French Underground. Jaunty, squinting fellows in berets with submachine guns slung over their leather jackets, sharing their wine and bread and cheese with you, and of course there'll have to be a girl, won't there — let's make her a famished little French girl who's been getting laid by a German Occupation officer and feeling perfectly awful about it — and you'll meet her at sunset in a beet field or a turnip field or some damn thing, and that night she'll come crawling into your sleeping bag, and oh, God, Jean-Paul, you make me want to throw up."

He didn't know what to say, but it seemed important to get to his feet, turn away, pull on his pants and fasten them. With his back to her, he said "Well, Alice, if you want to throw up I expect you'd better get into the bathroom first. Otherwise, I think it's probably time to put on your clothes and go home."

Then he risked a look at her. She was standing at the liquor table, trying to fix a drink, but her hands weren't steady enough for that because she was crying. The dark, ragged pout of her pubic thatch turned and stared at him. Did women realize how vulnerable, how pitiable that most prized and secret part of them could make them look, at moments like this? Probably so; they probably realized everything.

"Oh," she said. "Oh." And there was nothing to do but take her in his arms and let her weep against his chest. That seemed to make her feel better, and it made him feel fine: it was exactly how he'd planned to conclude the evening in the first place.

"Jean-Paul?" she asked, between sniffles.

"Mm?"

"Will they give you any training or anything? Before they start dropping you in behind enemy lines?"

The paperwork took very little time, and the commission came through in the last week of school before Christmas.

Alcott Knoedler was barely able to hide his irritation at the news — how and where could he find a new French teacher in the middle of the year? — but he managed to recover his sense of decorum in time for the day's assembly.

"One of our masters and friends," he announced, "has volunteered to serve his adopted nation. Mr. Jean-Paul La Prade today accepts a commission as captain in the United States Army. I congratulate him personally, as I know we all will, and I know we'll all wish him well. Mr. La Prade? Jean-Paul? Will you stand up back there please?"

This was ridiculous. La Prade had to rise from the seated faculty and stand in a sea of applause while a hundred and twenty-five pink young faces came swivelling around to smile at him over the backs of chairs. It was as if he were Louie Brundels, called from the kitchen on Thanksgiving Day; and the worst part, the awful part, was that it brought a quick warm swelling to the walls of his throat. My God, he thought, my God, I'm going to cry. What saved him, as he crouched and turned briefly right and left to acknowledge the clapping of his colleagues on either side, was a glimpse of Jack Draper's pale withered hands trying to clap along with the others, probably making no sound.

Chapter 5

Grove spent most of that Christmas vacation teaching himself to smoke. He would soon turn seventeen, and he didn't want to be the fool of the Senior Club.

First he had to learn the physical side of it — how to inhale without coughing; how to will his senses to accept drugged dizziness as pleasure rather than incipient nausea. Then came the subtler lessons in aesthetics, aided by the use of the bathroom mirror: learning to handle a cigarette casually, even gesturing with it while talking, as if scarcely aware of having it in his fingers; deciding which part of his lips formed the spot where a cigarette might hang most attractively — front and profile — and how best to squint against the smoke in both of those views. The remarkable thing about cigarettes, he discovered, was that they added years to the face that had always looked nakedly younger than his age.

By the time of his seventeenth birthday he was ready. His smoking passed the critical scrutiny of his peers — nobody laughed — and so he was initiated.

The Senior Club opened new horizons for all its members. It was a long, wide room with a flagstone floor, converted from one of the unused study halls of Four building. There was a pool table that seemed always to be in use, there were deep leather sofas and chairs, there was a phonograph with many records and a carefully neat display of current magazines. There was a big stone fireplace, too, and the pungent smell of woodsmoke, combining with the blue tobacco haze as the billiard balls clicked, gave flavor to everyone's sense of maturity. Only rarely did anything shrill or silly occur in the Senior Club; it was a place for learning how to behave in college — except, of course, that neither the class of '43 nor that of '44 could make plans for college until after the war.

"There's little or no training," Larry Gaines explained to a cluster of attentive listeners around the fireplace one afternoon. "It's not like a regular branch of the service at all. You sign on and you ship out; that's about it."

Larry Gaines had tried to enlist in the Army, the Marine Corps, and the Navy — he had been ready to leave school at once for any of them — but they'd all turned him down because of an obscure physical ailment he'd never known he had. Now he had settled for his last resort, the Merchant Marine — and the Merchant Marine, which might otherwise have seemed drab and spiritless, was beginning to take on an aura of romance at Dorset Academy because of him.

At the urging of Pop Driscoll and others he had agreed not to sign on and ship out right away, but he'd arranged with the dean to take his final exams and get his diploma a month ahead of time, so he could leave early in May.

"And of course there's no uniform or anything," he was saying. "Just regular work clothes; you buy your own. Except I imagine the guys keep dress clothes in their lockers too, so they can show a little class around the girls in Algiers, or wherever they're going. Ah, look, I'm probably making it sound better than it is. It's probably the most boring life in the world, chipping paint all day, and stuff like that, but what the hell; it's the best I can do. Listen, I've gotta cut out. See you guys later."

Larry Gaines never spent much time hanging around the Senior Club, though he could always command a respectful audience there. He was President of the Student Council now, and there seemed always to be matters that required his attention. "See you guys later," he would say, and disappear into his responsibilities.

"Hey, Grove?" Pierre Van Loon said in the darkness of their double room that night. "You awake?"

"Yeah."

"Know something? The way Gaines was talking today, about the Merchant Marine and all — that really sounded nice."

"How do you mean?"

"Ah, I don't know; it just did. Be out working in the sun, chipping paint or whatever it is you have to do for maybe a couple of weeks at sea, then pull into someplace like Algiers and go to hell with yourself. I guess you don't see what I mean."

"Well, I think I do, sort of."

"Because the point is, kids in private schools don't know

anything about reality. Look: I figure I've got about a year
left before the Army gets me, and you know what I'd like to
do? Oh, I probably won't *do* this, because my parents'd kill
me, at least my father would, but I'd like to spend the whole
year bumming around this country. Out to the West Coast
and back, with side trips along the way. And I'd never pay
for transportation: I'd hitchhike or I'd ride the freights.
When I hit the oil fields I'd sign on as a roughneck. You know
what a roughneck is?"

"Yeah, I've heard about that."

"Then when I got into the cattle country I'd work as a
cowhand. I can ride. And wherever they're building high-
ways, I'd work as a hard-rock miner. You know what a hard-
rock miner is?"

"I think I can figure it out."

"Well, but do you see, the point is I'd always be moving on;
moving on. Go broke, take a job for a while, hit the road
again. And there'd be girls! Jesus, Grove, think of the *girls*.
And I'd just be the lonesome stranger, always moving on."

"Yeah," Grove said. "Well, if you can't do something like
that now, I guess there won't be much chance of doing it
until after the war."

"Oh, I know," Van Loon said. "But after the war, boy, I'm
really gonna — that's really what I'm gonna do."

"Gentlemen," W. Alcott Knoedler said to his assembled faculty, "I wish I had encouraging news this afternoon, but I
won't lie to you. We're in trouble."

They were gathered in the extravagantly spacious living
room of the headmaster's residence — a room that embarrassed Knoedler's wife ("What can I *do* in there, Alcott?")
and took young girls' breath away when they first walked

into it in their evening gowns, on the arms of their "dates," for the annual Spring Dance. Old Mrs. Hooper had stocked the long panelled walls with thousands of leather-bound books whose pages would never be cut, and with oil portraits of worthy-looking men and women whom no one could identify. Except perhaps at the Spring Dance, when the kids did seem to have a pretty good time, it was a place of anxiety — a room where you sat and waited and found that your palms were damp in meetings like this.

"Like all private schools, we rely on tuition as our primary source of income," Knoedler said. "In the past, from time to time, we've been able to draw on funds made available by Mrs. Hooper's foundation, but that source is closed to us now. For reasons of her own, Mrs. Hooper has made clear that she plans no further financial aid.

"With a small enrollment, and with many of the boys paying half tuition, we can't begin to meet our costs. We've been operating at a deficit for some years, and we've reached a point of crisis.

"I met with the board of trustees last week, and a suggestion was made which I'll pass along to you now. If each member of the faculty were to accept a voluntary cut in salary as a temporary measure — oh, perhaps twenty-five percent — we might well be able to remain solvent."

And they turned him down. Dr. Wilson, the old history master, was the first to speak: he said he couldn't possibly absorb a twenty-five percent salary cut, and added that he didn't see why the faculty should be made to suffer for Mrs. Hooper's intransigence; then Dr. Stone spoke up in agreement, and because everybody knew that Edgar Stone was the highest-paid man on the staff it was easy to follow his lead. The refusal was unanimous.

"All right, gentlemen," Knoedler said, "I've presented the

board's recommendation and I've noted your response. I see no point in prolonging this meeting. I'll keep you informed of any new developments."

On leaving the headmaster's house, Robert Driscoll held himself down to a toddler's stroll in order to walk beside Jack Draper. It was on the tip of his tongue to say "How're things at home, Jack?" but he thought better of it and cast about for other things to say instead. For several months now, since La Prade had gone, he'd been nagged with curiosity about how the Drapers were getting along. Had they just sort of fallen back into sleeping together again? Was that what people did? Or were there terrible scenes at night with tears and recriminations and heavy drinking and talk of divorce, until Jack passed out on the living-room sofa and the children came down and found him there in the morning?

"Jack?" he said. "Marge and I were saying just last night that we hardly ever see you anymore. Why don't you and Alice come over for a drink some night this week?"

Draper's walk, as well as being very slow, required him to move his arms in a trembling parody of a British soldier on parade. His head, erect and tense now in the effort of walking, was small and handsome, with close-cut blond hair beginning to recede at the temples. Even before the polio he must have been a slight man, but it had probably been the kind of slightness many women admire. "Well, thanks, Bob, that's nice," he said. "I'll give you a call in a couple of days, okay?"

Then Driscoll left him, and Draper continued to make his laborious way home. He was passing through the bleak, sandy area behind Four building now, where the unfinished foundations lay like ruins. Why had they set the science building and the science masters' houses so far away from

the main part of the school? Had some mordant architect
guessed there might one day be a science master barely able
to walk the distance? Or maybe they had somehow predicted, those fanciful "Cotswold" architects of Mrs. Hooper's,
that there might one day be a houseful of pain out there
beyond the sand — a cuckold's house so steeped in loss that
even the children's smiles were sad.

"Jack?" Alice called from the next room. "Was there anything new?"

"Anything new?"

"You know; about the school folding up."

"Oh. No."

At first, soon after La Prade's departure, Jack Draper had
been torn with wondering what his wife would do. Come
back to him? Take the children and leave him? The next
move seemed plainly up to her, and she had refused and
refused to make her position clear.

"I have to think," she had explained. "I have to take stock.
I have to work a few things out in my mind."

Well, okay, but what exactly did all that mean? Think
about what? Take stock of what? Work *what* things out in
her mind?

And now it was spring. In the evenings, after dinner and
before the children's bedtime, the four of them would sit
around the living room in simulation of what real families
might be expected to do. He had to admit he was stiff with
drink on most of those occasions: he would usually start
drinking in the lab in the afternoon and keep it going with
heavy shots of bourbon in the kitchen before dinner, and
more afterwards.

"Why do your lips look all funny, Daddy?" Millicent asked
one night.

"My lips? I don't know; maybe it's because I need a kiss."

Another time he said something dry and witty to his son
— he couldn't even remember what it was — and Alice's
sweet face fell apart in laughter. Her big, lovely eyes danced
briefly for him on her side of the room; just before turning
away again she said "That's funny, Jack."

And that took him back to a time long ago, in college, when
a man of much-admired worldliness had said "Know something, Jack? You'll find there's no greater pleasure in life
than making a girl laugh. Apart from getting laid itself, of
course."

Of course. Getting laid itself. And having now made a girl
laugh, was it wholly unreasonable to imagine he might have
improved his chances in the area of getting laid itself?
Wasn't getting laid itself a thing almost everyone deserved?
Wasn't it what made the world go around? Even for a funny
little polio victim whose arms and legs didn't really amount
to arms and legs at all, and whose wife had been fucked out
of her mind by a Frenchman for a year and a half?

But every night, as he struggled out of his Brooks Brothers
clothes — oh, yes, and fuck you too, Brooks Brothers, with
the terribly tactful bastards in your fitting room ("I expect
you'll want it taken in quite a bit here, sir, am I right? And
the trousers taken in quite a bit here? Am I right? And
here?") — every night, as Jack Draper crawled wretchedly
naked into his marriage bed, he knew his wife would not join
him there. He even knew, with a cripple's resignation and a
drunkard's terrible calm, that she would probably never join
him there again.

Hugh Britt sometimes complained that his leg was "acting
up"; he would sit in the *Chronicle* office kneading the thigh
muscles with one strong hand while he winced in pain and

blew thin, fatalistic jets of cigarette smoke that billowed back from the open pages of *The Brothers Karamazov.*

"Is that any good?" Grove asked him once.

And Britt looked up in irritation. "What do you mean, 'any good'? It's one of the great works of all time."

"Yeah, well, what I really mean is, how come you can read it when your leg hurts? I mean, when I'm in pain I just want to lie down and wait for it to be over. See what I mean?"

"Grove, there are times when I simply *don't* see what you mean. If I were to lie down now I'd be screaming, or tearing the pillow to shreds with my teeth. I happen to have a good power of concentration and I'm grateful for it in situations like this. Reading takes my mind off the pain."

"Oh." And Grove went back to his half-written editorial. It had started off well enough, something about how "our men overseas" might wish for Dorset Academy to become "a better school than the school we know," but in trying to bring that idea around to a conclusion he had messed up the whole damn thing twice. He knew he could probably write smarter editorials if he read *The Brothers Karamazov* and some of the other great works of all time, but there was the trouble: if he sat around reading the great works of all time, in or out of pain, how would he ever get his editorials written?

Then Bucky Ward came into the office, dragging a ten- or twelve-foot length of twine with many tin cans attached to it.

"I thought this might be interesting," he said. "We could tie it to the back of Knoedler's car and he might not notice it until he's on the road."

"You know something, Ward?" Britt said. "That's the kind of thing people do when they're nine or ten years old."

"Yeah, well, I guess I'm slow in the head, then. Always

knew there was something funny upstairs. Listen, though, you want to do this, Bill, or not? Because if not I'll throw it away."

"Leave it here under the desk for now, okay?" Grove said. "I've got to finish this damn thing."

"Take your time," Ward said, and he assumed a self-conscious saunter, holding his shoulders high, as he left the room. "No hurry at all."

All winter, and well into the spring, Grove had been in the quandary of having two friends who didn't much like each other. Sometimes it seemed that he couldn't really consider Britt a friend — how could anything as warm and sloppy as friendship apply to an ice-cold perfectionist like Britt? — but he had to acknowledge that Britt was still the one person in the world whose approval he wanted most. And there were signs that he might soon win it, if he watched his step and didn't fall into dumb stuff like asking if *The Brothers Karamazov* was any good. Several times Britt had expressed distaste for his present roommate, the plump Kimball, whose bed quaked in its frame every night with the vigor of his masturbation ("I don't think he cares whether I hear it or *not,* for God's sake") and more than once he had left an implication, too vague to be pressed, that he might be open to the idea of rooming with Grove next year.

As for Bucky Ward, it couldn't be denied that the fine companionship of last fall had begun to dwindle as soon as Britt got out of the infirmary. It was strengthened from time to time — there were still long nights in the *Chronicle* office when they were hilarious or sad together, depending on Ward's mood — but it was troubled now, at best, and that seemed to be one of the things that made Ward sad.

"Is Britt supposed to be one of these terrifically intelligent guys?" he asked Grove one night. "Very high I.Q. and all that?"

"I don't know. He certainly gets good grades."

"Yeah. Well, sometimes getting good grades is really just a trick, like any other kind of success. It's a habit of mind. All you have to do is shut out the rest of the world."

"How do you mean, shut out the rest of the world? Britt doesn't do that. He plays football, he works on the paper, he — "

"Oh, Jesus, Grove, come on. You mean you really don't see what I mean?" And Bucky Ward gazed down with a rueful little smile. "Okay. Okay. If you don't see what I mean, there's certainly no point in my trying to explain it to you." After a while he said "Damn. Sometimes talking to you is like talking to my girl."

"What the hell do you mean by that?"

"Well, both you and Polly are perfectly bright, and you look at everything, but a lot of the time you don't see what you're looking at. And I mean I love Polly and I like you, but there are all these things you don't *see*. Ah, never mind. Never mind. Let's forget it."

After Ward had left his string of tin cans in the office that afternoon, Britt looked up thoughtfully from *The Brothers Karamazov* and said "Know something, Grove? I think your friend Bucky's got a few problems. He can't seem to decide whether to be a silly kid playing pranks or some kind of thundering Jesus in a hair shirt. Pretty strange set of alternatives."

"Yeah."

"Oh, I suppose it goes back to his being sick so much as a kid, but even so. The excuse of an unhappy childhood can only take you so far."

"Yeah."

"And he really seems like a spoiled brat to me, a lot of the time. I mean I like him, but he has that spoiled-brat quality."

"Yeah," Grove said, "but look — " And he was surprised to hear himself saying this; it was like something Britt ought to be saying to him. " — look, could we talk about it later? Because I mean I've really got to finish this fucking editorial."

Terry Flynn had told Jim Pomeroy once, early in their friendship, that the reason for his being two years behind in school was that his family had changed homes so often during his childhood. "We were always moving," he explained, "because of my dad's business. I'd just be getting settled in one school and wham, we'd move again, sometimes in the middle of a school year, so I just sort of naturally fell behind."

"I see," Pomeroy said, but the more he thought about it, especially after they started rooming together, the clearer it became that he didn't really see at all.

As the months went by, with Terry coming into the room after each school day and planking down his idiotic third-form textbooks on the window ledge beside Pomeroy's fifth-form books, there was an increasing tension in the air.

"Terry?" Pomeroy inquired one evening, while Flynn stood scrutinizing his mirror for facial blemishes. "Listen, what's the main thing that's holding you back in school? You mind my asking you that?"

"Well, it's mainly my reading," Flynn said — and he said it in the shy, divulging way that an artist might say "my painting" or a composer might say "my music," or a crippled man, like Mr. Draper, "my legs."

His reading? How could anybody's *reading* matter that

much? What the hell was there about *reading* that could mess up your life?

"I have a problem with reading, you see," Flynn explained. "It's better this year — it's getting better all the time — but there's still a problem. I never really learned to read well when I was a kid, you see, because of all the moving around, and so it's become a — you know — it's become a problem. But it's getting better."

"Oh," Jim Pomeroy said, and his mind went away to all the other people he knew at Dorset Academy who could read without thinking about it. Wasn't everybody, for Christ's sake, supposed to be able to read without thinking about it? Take Steve MacKenzie, who could stand alone in Pop Driscoll's class and deliver every word of Kipling's "If" from memory. Damn, damn, that had been a fine performance. Or take Lear, whose rich English accent, when he was called upon to read aloud from *The Merchant of Venice* ("Sit, Jessica. Look how the floor of heaven is thick inlaid with patines of bright gold . . .") had suddenly brought the whole fucking play alive for a roomful of slobs who only minutes before had been in unanimous, grumbling agreement that Shakespeare was impossible to understand. Or take Grove, running around and scribbling all day, getting the paper out on time every two weeks — never failing — and seeing to it that its columns really did make sense, in real printed type, for people to read. Damn.

"Well, Terry," Pomeroy said, "Why do you suppose you have this trouble with reading?"

"I've told you. My parents moved around a lot, and I — "

"Yeah, yeah," Pomeroy said, "but a lot of people's parents move around. I mean mine didn't, but plenty of others do. So I mean what do you really think is the — "

"Look, Jim." Terry Flynn turned quickly from the mirror and stood glaring, his eyes bright, with sudden touches of pink in both cheeks. "I really don't want to talk about this anymore, okay?"

Well, okay and okay and okay. They didn't talk about it anymore. But Jim Pomeroy, who'd been told more than once that he might be a strong candidate for next year's Student Council (and wouldn't that be a nice thing to have in your life, before being swallowed up in the Army?) — somebody like Jim Pomeroy could hardly be expected to put up forever with a dumbbell kid who didn't even know how to read.

Another time, in the spring, Pomeroy failed to come back to the room one afternoon — he had to take his shower later, after study hall — and when Flynn finally saw him that night he said "Where were you?"

"Whaddya mean, where was I? Where was I when?"

"You know. This afternoon."

"Oh, I don't know; Steve MacKenzie and I were out in front of One building for a while, throwing a baseball around. We weren't watching the time."

"Oh."

And that seemed to take care of it, though neither of them spoke again until Lights. Then, in the darkness of the small room, Flynn said "Jim?"

"Yeah?"

"Want to talk a while, or just go to sleep?"

"I don't know, Terry; I'm pretty tired tonight, as a matter of fact."

That was another thing: Terry Flynn seemed to think that being roommates meant you had to lie there talking and giggling every night like a couple of — well, hell, like a couple of girls. Pomeroy rolled over and punched his pillow and tried to settle down. But sleep was held at bay by the chance that at any moment Terry's voice might say, from across the room, "Jim? . . . Jim? . . ." When he finally did drift off into a kind of floating half-sleep, it was only to be assaulted by a dream in which Terry appeared, smiling and saying "Look what *I've* got," holding up first a child's chaotic fingerpainting, then another big sheet of kindergarten art paper on which several cutouts of orange jack-o'-lanterns had been sloppily pasted. "See?" Terry said. "See what I can do? Bubba-*hah!* Bubba-hah-*hah!*"

Pomeroy fought himself awake; then, grateful to know it had only been a dream, he breathed very slowly, dimly aware of similar breathing across the room, until he began to notice the sweet scent of Terry's deodorant cream. Nobody else he knew used stuff like that. He had never understood why Terry did, and hadn't found a way to ask, and the smell of it, up close, was enough to make him faintly ill. Oh, Jesus; oh, Jesus; life was a pain in the ass.

A week or two later, at shower time one day, Terry Flynn came hurrying out of the steam and down the hall after Pomeroy, calling "Jim? Jim?"

"Yeah?"

"Wait. Listen. You're not mad at me, are you?"

"Whaddya mean, 'mad' at you?"

"Well, you know; just now, in the showers, when I said that about Steve MacKenzie. I hope you didn't think I — "

"Oh, for Christ's sake, Flynn," Pomeroy said. "Whaddya think I am, some girl?" Back in their room he whipped off his towel, struggled into his underpants and then his pants and then his shirt, breathing hard.

Flynn was getting dressed too, on his own side of the room, but more slowly. He kept glancing over at Pomeroy as if to make sure everything was still all right between them.

Both fully dressed, they found there was well over an hour left before dinner, with nothing to do but sit there and look at each other.

"Want to talk?" Flynn inquired shyly.

"What about?"

"I don't know; just — you know — whatever you feel like."

"Terry, listen," Pomeroy said. "I've been thinking. It seems to me we talk too much. We talk all the damn time. I think we'd both be better off if we just sort of shut up and went about our business."

There was a long silence while Flynn stared at his own tightly clasped hands. Then he looked up and said, "You don't want to be friends anymore?"

"I didn't *say* that. Christ's sake, Flynn, you can take the simplest thing and twist it around into the God damndest — listen. Listen. I simply said I think we *talk* too much, that's all, and I get *tired* of it, that's all, and I think anybody listening to us'd think we were a couple of fucking *girls*, that's all. Now, let's forget it."

"Okay," Flynn said after a while. "You want me to move out, then, so you can get Steve MacKenzie in here. Okay. Okay. I know how you feel about Steve MacKenzie and I know how you feel about me. It's perfectly okay with me, Jim, but I want to tell you something." He was on his feet, trembling. There was a bright terrible welling of tears in his eyes, and his mouth had begun to twitch into uncontrollable shapes. "I want to tell you something. Steve MacKenzie's a prick. Steve MacKenzie's a prick. Steve MacKenzie's a prick."

"Ah, fuck you, Flynn," Pomeroy said. "That's all I've got to say, now or ever. Fuck you." And he waited only long enough to see Terry Flynn turn away and crouch over his bed — to see, horrified, that the back of Terry's best tweed

Brooks Brothers jacket was shaking with sobs — before he
slammed out of the room.

At least four or five guys were standing there in the
hall — God only knew how many guys had heard everything
— and they all gave him funny, half-smiling looks as he
made his furious way to the stairwell. Yeah, well, fuck you
too, he almost said aloud.

But down in the quadrangle, walking out under the trees
on the hard, satisfying flagstones, he began to feel better.
The thing was done. The mission was accomplished. Unless
Flynn really did move out, which wasn't likely (even Flynn
would be able to see the pathos in dismantling the yellow
curtains and taking down the eight New England scenes),
they could probably survive the rest of the spring together
as cordial strangers. There would be no more wistful appeals
for "talk" now, nor any bleating down the corridor of "Jim?
Jim?"

It was over. Pomeroy felt so exultant he wanted to dance
on the flagstone path. He was free. And next year he could
take a room with — well, with Steve MacKenzie, if they both
felt like it. Why not?

Grove usually liked the printshop on days when they were
making up the paper: he enjoyed his authority over the
younger boys, and his status of near-equality with Mr. Gold.
And he liked the shop itself — the warm, dry smells of it, and
the sight of his own words gleaming upside down and back-
wards in the long galleys of linotype.

But one afternoon nothing seemed to go right. He was late
for work, which brought on a quiet little flood of sarcasm
from Mr. Gold that made two of the younger boys laugh;
then later Mr. Gold looked gloomily up from the composing

table and said "Grove, I think we're running short. We can
use the 'Buy War Bonds' box on page four, but I'm worried
about page three." Mr. Gold was always worried, either that
there was too little material or too much.

"It'll be all right," Grove told him. "There's enough stuff."

"Well, I don't know why these things can't be planned a
little more accurately. We'll be lucky if we ever get out of
here tonight."

Somehow, all the page forms were filled and locked and
ready for printing at the accostomed time. Mr. Gold, with a
varnished dollar pipe clenched cold in his mouth, stood
moodily feeding the big, fast platen press; the boys could
leave now, and as Grove made for the door he didn't care if
he ever saw the printshop again.

Outside, he singled out one of the younger boys and drew
him aside against a red stone wall to ask him a question. It
was Dwight Reeves, the boy who'd come blinking out of
Henry Weaver's room one night and been called a punk,
more than a year ago.

"Tell me something, Reeves," Grove said. "What *were* you
and Weaver doing up there that night?"

"Up where? What night?" And Reeves blushed, which was
gratifying.

"Come on. You know. Last year."

"We were wrestling."

"Wrestling?"

"Well, wrestling," Reeves said, and then he added a shy,
simpering qualification that he might always regret. "And
maybe a little something else."

"Oh," Grove said, "maybe a little something else." And he
drew his mouth to one side in a way that he hoped would
express revulsion. "Okay."

His afternoon in the printshop had badly depressed him

(there had been a perilous moment when he'd felt his eyes sting from Mr. Gold's sarcasm and the younger boys' laughter) and his interview with Reeves had only made it worse. The only thing to do now was head for the Senior Club, where it was sometimes possible to feel almost grown up.

In good weather, some Club members liked to sit outside behind Four building on a long wooden bench against the wall. They could meditatively spit in the dust at their feet, or they could hunch with their forearms on their knees and their cigarettes dangling, ready to stare down whatever younger boys might approach and pass by on their way to the Four building archway. This afternoon Pierre Van Loon was alone on the bench; he was engaged in what looked like an earnest conversation with one of the white-clad kitchen help, who stood a few feet away and pawed the sand with one broken black shoe.

"Hi, Grove," Van Loon said. "This is my friend Wayne. Bill Grove, Wayne."

"Hi," Grove said.

"Hey." Wayne's age could have been anything from twenty-five to forty — younger than most of the kitchen help — and he had a guarded look that Grove found vaguely frightening.

"Wayne's from West Virginia," Van Loon said. "Got tired of coal mining, so he came up here. He's a good friend of Ed and Mary Slovak."

"Who?"

"Ed Slovak, works down at the power plant, and his wife Mary. *I've* told you about them."

And Grove did remember. On several nights, coming back to the dormitory just in time for Lights, Van Loon had announced that he'd been out visiting the Slovaks, great people, and that they'd served him bourbon whiskey. Ed Slovak might have been a great engineer if he'd had the education, but he wasn't bitter; that was the great thing about him. Mary wasn't bitter either. They were just — well, they were interesting people. And now, apparently, Van Loon had found another candidate for his widening social circle among the school employees.

"Wayne's only working here until he gets a little money together," he explained. "Then he's going to try his luck in Canada."

"I see," Grove said.

"I was just telling him I think he'll be making a wise move," Van Loon said, carefully flicking the ash from his cigarette. "Canada's the country of the future."

"Yeah, I guess that's right."

Wayne said something inaudible.

"How's that, Wayne?" Van Loon asked him.

"I said the main thing's to keep movin'."

"Right. Yeah, you're absolutely right about that."

The talk petered out then; Wayne went upstairs to his quarters and Van Loon leaned back against Four building with a sigh. "I don't suppose you understand this, Grove," he said, "but I'm interested in people like that. I'm interested in all kinds of people, not just the kids you meet in a private school."

"Yeah."

"Know what I'd really like to do? For the next year, before the Army gets me? I'd like to spend the whole year bumming around this country."

"Yeah, I know," Grove said. "You've told me about that."

They went in to the Club together just as Lear and Jennings were coming out. "You going over to the Stones?" Lear inquired.

"No."

"Too bad," Lear said. "It's another gala afternoon. Edith's home."

"She is?" Grove said. "Again?"

"Ah, yes, she keeps on coming home and coming home, and no one can explain it. I have my own theory, though." And Lear carefully straightened his tie. He had recently begun encouraging people to call him by the spelling of his first three initials — "Ret" — probably because it suggested Rhett Butler in *Gone With the Wind*. "I think she comes home to see me," he said.

Chapter  6

When anyone asked her how she liked Miss Blair's, Edith Stone said it was very nice. This wasn't true at all.

She didn't like the dormitory, which smelled of caramels and throbbed with talk of menstruation and virginity; she didn't like the sweat and clatter and clumsy exertion of field hockey; she didn't like any of her courses or any of the other girls.

There were several girls who admired her and sought her approval, but they laughed too much and they all wanted to talk about the same boring, boring, boring things; and there were no girls whom she admired or whose approval she sought.

"*Dorset Academy?*" they would cry on hearing where her father taught, and then they would giggle behind their hands in order to leave no doubt of their opinion that Dorset was a funny school. "Well," one of them said once, in a tone of forgiveness, "it can't be all bad if Gus Gerhardt goes there; he's a living dream."

And that stayed in Edith's mind the next time she was home. Sitting beside her father in the refectory, she considered asking him to point out Gus Gerhardt to her, but decided it would be silly. Besides, she had only to glance around this table to see any number of perfectly nice, presentable boys, several of whom could be counted on for shy conversation if she felt like talking. Only a year ago she had hated these refectory dinners at Dorset; now she looked forward to them. She liked the occasional afternoon teas with her mother, too: the guests usually included a witty English boy named Rhett Lear, who could make her laugh, and a big, bashful boy named Art Jennings who blushed a lot; and once an extraordinary-looking boy had dropped in for a few minutes, drawing everyone's attention, making her weak and dumb until he smiled at her and introduced himself as Larry Gaines.

Still, she had to spend nine-tenths of her time in the oppressive tedium of Miss Blair's. Brushing her hair a hundred strokes on each side every night, she would often stare into the mirror with a sense of helplessness.

No matter how she held it, her face wasn't quite right. It had a nice oval shape on a long neck, her brown eyes were set well apart, and her mouth, though possibly too big, was of the kind called "sensual"; the trouble was in her chin. It didn't jut. It wasn't "pert." It didn't have the delicately firm, bony look of chins in every pretty face she had ever seen.

Turning, examining her profile with a hand mirror, she could only hate the sight of it.

"You're a *lovely* girl, Edith," her mother would say; but then, everybody's mother said stuff like that. Besides, her mother had a decent chin; even the most terrible girls at Miss Blair's had decent chins, so there was nothing to do but drop the hairbrush and the hand mirror on her bureau and pace the floor of her room with both small fists at her temples.

On other nights the mirror was more agreeable. Then she was sometimes able to see a romantic, even a mysterious girl there, a girl who didn't mind letting a heavy lock of hair fall over half her face because throwing it back only emphasized the sparkle in the deep browns and whites of her eyes, the subtle shape of her generous, sensual mouth and the proud column of her neck. At times like that even her chin looked all right. And she would picture the apartment she planned to have as soon as possible, either in Cambridge or New York: a high, white room with a guitar hung on the wall above the studio couch (she didn't yet know how to play a guitar, but there'd be time for everything). There would be a fireplace, too, and a coffee table with a wooden bowl of oranges, and she would move gracefully around wearing sandals, a man's shirt with the top several buttons unfastened, and a full skirt — or better still, a pair of close-fitting, well-faded blue jeans ("You ought to wear jeans more often, Edith," one of the girls had told her; "they look really sexy on you").

One afternoon when the weight of Miss Blair's seemed too great to be borne, she took a navel orange off her bureau and left the dormitory and walked out across the campus, crunching raked pebbles decisively under her heels, offering only the most cursory nods of greeting to everyone she passed. She wanted to get away.

There was a place she had gone to before at times like this, a grassy knoll hidden by trees from all the distant windows of the school and overlooking one of the huge, flat lawns that kept the campus away from the world. Sitting here, with her legs tucked up under her skirt, using the nails of her thumbs to peel her orange, she could be reasonably sure of privacy. All day she'd had difficulty in breathing. Her lungs felt tense and shallow, as if she might have to gasp for breath at any moment.

Slowly, so as to make it last, she began separating the segments of the orange and picking off the little white shreds from each one before eating it. She dried her fingers in the grass beside her thigh, and that made her think of a poet she had recently discovered named Edna St. Vincent Millay.

> *God, I can push the grass apart*
> *And lay my finger on your heart.*

"Well, I suppose that kind of thing can be affecting at your age," her father had said in the dry, tolerant, infuriating way that ruined all the talks they ever had about books. "Later on, I expect you'll grow impatient with sentimentality; most bright people do."

"Well, but I mean what do you *mean*, sentimentality, Daddy?"

And he had reached out to tousle her hair as if she were six instead of sixteen. "What do you *mean*, you mean what do I mean sentimentality?" he said. "What's the meaning of meaning? Ever think of that?"

"Oh, your father's impossible," her mother had said with a shudder. "Your father's so jaded and distant and cold he doesn't like anybody at all. He doesn't even like Alice Duer *Miller.*"

"Well," Edith said, because it always seemed necessary to clear the air in that house, "as a matter of fact I don't much like Alice Duer Miller either, Mother."

And that caused her mother to look stricken. "Have you no heart, then? Have you lost your heart, like everyone else I've ever loved? Am I doomed, Edith? Am I doomed to die alone? Tell me. Tell me the truth. I can't live with lies."

What was the meaning of meaning? As she chewed and swallowed the last of her orange, she stared out over the enormous lawn and watched the slow approach of a tractor pulling a rig of mowers in what was probably the first lawn-mowing job of the year. The tractor shimmered and gave off a sound disproportionate to its size, a harsh thrumming that suited her mood because it suggested the ugliness of the world. The old German groundskeeper, Mr. Gerhardt, rode hunched over the wheel with the stub of a cigar in his dumb, grumpy mouth. Everything, everything was ugly; there was no peace to be found even on this grass, beneath these trees.

She had just gotten to her feet to go back to the dorm, because there was nothing else to do, when a Model T Ford pulled up to a stop on the road beside the lawn and a broad-shouldered boy got out, wearing jeans and a blazing white T-shirt. He walked up to the idling tractor and said something to Mr. Gerhardt, who left the engine running and climbed down. There was a brief conference; then the boy swung up onto the tractor and put it into gear, and the old man plodded out to the car and drove away.

It had to be Gus Gerhardt. And all at once it became very important for Edith to get a closer look at him. She hurried down the slope and began walking. He was still many yards away, coming toward her; there was time to compose herself, and she willed her legs to slow down to a stroll. She could make out his blond, frowning face now, and as he came up close she stopped, smiled, and waved to him.

He gave her a hesitant, doubtful look; then the terrible noise of the tractor swept past her in a great smell of gasoline, with the mowers racketing along behind it, and she was standing on cropped grass in which bugs were jumping. After a moment he brought his machinery to a stop, cut the engine and turned around in the high iron seat to peer back at her.

"Did you want something?" he called.

"No, no; that's all right; I just — "

"Huh?"

And all she could do was walk toward him over the stubble, feeling like a fool. "I just wanted to say hello, that's all," she said when they were within speaking distance. "I think I may have seen you a few times, over at Dorset. I'm Edith Stone."

"Oh, yeah." His smile was a fraction of a second too slow in breaking, and it looked guarded even then. "Yeah, I've seen you too sometimes, in the refectory. Only thing is I didn't — you know — didn't recognize you."

For what seemed at least ten seconds they had nothing to say. "Do you — work over here often?" she asked at last.

"Once in a while," he said. "Whenever there's — you know — whenever my father needs the help."

"Well, there certainly must be a — lot of work to do around a place like this."

"Yeah. Well."

"Well. Nice to see you."

"Yeah." And the noise of the tractor was deafening as he pulled slowly away. There was no peace in the world; there was no beauty; there was no air to breathe; there was nothing at all.

That Friday, in her parents' house, Edith went to bed at four o'clock in the afternoon and stayed there for twenty-four hours.

At intervals, her mother would tiptoe into the room with anxious looks. "Dear, are you sure you don't want me to call the doctor?"

"No. I mean yes, I'm sure."

"Well, but what do you suppose it could be?"

"I told you. It's nothing. I just don't happen to feel like getting up."

"But you haven't eaten anything at all since — "

"I may have a glass of milk later on."

"Oh, Edith. You're having one of your things, aren't you."

"I don't know. I really don't feel too much like talking, Mother."

At last, when it was teatime on the second day, her mother came in looking bright and pretty and a little distracted, as if by flirtation. "Some of the boys are downstairs, Edith," she said, "and I know they'd like to see you. Why don't you get up and come join us."

Edith rolled heavily away to face the wall, dragging the wrinkled bedclothes behind her.

"Oh, come on," her mother said. "You'll feel better in no time. Lear's here, I know you like him, and Jennings, and a few others — oh, and Larry Gaines is here too."

Edith rolled back, hoping the eagerness wouldn't show in her face, and said she guessed she might be down in a little while.

"Oh, good. They'll be so pleased."

As she hurried through a hot shower and then into the best dress she could find, Edith's heart beat so soundly and rapidly she could only assume that this was what happened when you rushed into activity after too long a rest; she had to stand at the top of the stairs for a long time, breathing hard, holding the newel post with both hands, before she felt calm enough to go down.

There was a great stirring of tweed and flannel as five or six boys got to their feet; there were bashful smiles and a ragged chorus of "Hi, Edith" — and there he was, looking older and more manly than any of the others, his head made golden in the afternoon light: Larry Gaines.

"Can I get you some tea or something, Edith?" he said. Even then he seemed to know that she'd come down especially for him, that she wanted to talk to him, that she wanted to sit with him and watch his face.

When they were settled together, hesitantly sipping tea, the other boys might as well have vanished from the room. "I hear you'll be going into the service soon, Larry," she said.

"Well, it's not really the service; it's the Merchant Marine."

"I know. Do they train you for that?"

"Oh, not really. There's little or no training. You sign on and you ship out; that's about it." After a moment he said "I tried to enlist in all the regular branches, but they turned me down."

"I know," she said. "I heard that too. Everything you do becomes common knowledge very quickly around here; I'm sure you're aware of that."

And he blushed, just as if he were an ordinary boy, as if he weren't President of the Student Council and the most remarkable Dorset boy in anyone's memory. The surprising discovery that she could make him blush gave her a thrill of advantage, and she pressed it. "Well, maybe not *every*thing you do," she said. "I imagine even you must have a few secrets."

"Oh, I don't know." He had recovered from the blush and was looking at her in a keen, self-confident way that might have been infuriating if she hadn't liked him so much. "I don't think I have any secrets. If I did, I'd probably tell them to you."

"You would? Why?"

"Because you're so nice, and because you're such a pretty girl."

At dinner that night he let the whole refectory see that he'd abandoned his place at the sixth-form table in order to sit with her, beside her father.

"To what do we owe this honor, Larry?" her father inquired.

"To the beauty and charm of your daughter, Dr. Stone," he said.

Extraordinary things were happening to Edith. Sitting there, smiling and talking and forking down chicken-noodle casserole, she could feel the tingling surface of her skin down the whole length of her body, under her clothes; she could have sworn she felt her very womb opening up. The word "love" kept occurring to her. I'm falling in love, she thought. Oh God; oh God; I'm falling in love with Larry Gaines.

When dinner was over he didn't seem to mind anyone's noticing how he steered her clear of the crowd, walking with his warm hand cradling her elbow. Then he guided her away from the quadrangle, away from everyone, and out to the sandy area behind Four building, where he gathered her up close and kissed her on the mouth for a long time. In three weeks she would be seventeen, and this was the first time she had ever been kissed.

*   *   *

Larry Gaines was overwhelming. He was brilliant, he was handsome, he was good; there was too much of him for Edith to comprehend all at once. All she knew, daydreaming and sleepwalking through the requirements of her time at Miss Blair's during the next few days, was that she was in love.

"Oh, Larry," she rehearsed in whispers many times, "Oh, Larry, I love you."

She couldn't get home until the following Friday, and the ugly shock of that afternoon was that Larry Gaines didn't come to tea. He didn't come on Saturday, either, and one of the other boys explained that this was because he was busy with his duties as chairman of the Spring Dance committee. The dance was only a week away.

So now there were two terrible things to think about as she sat with her cooling tea in a roomful of adolescent boys: she might not get to see Larry Gaines all weekend; and next week he might well show up for the dance with some sleek, lovely girl from his home town.

The thought of her bed upstairs was dismally tempting — she could have another long rest — but if she missed dinner she would never know whether he might have come to sit at her father's table again.

". . . Excuse me; did you say something?" she said to a skinny boy in an awful suit.

"I just said I don't think we've met. My name's Bill Grove."

And she managed to talk to him for a while; it was probably better than keeping silent. He was nice in an awkward way, and so nervous — twisting his hands, shifting in his chair — that he made her feel calm.

"Do you have something to do with the student government?" she asked kindly, knowing he probably didn't.

"Oh, no," he said. "Nothing like that. I'm editor of the school paper, is all. The *Chronicle.*"

"Oh? Well, that must be very interesting."

"Yeah, well, it's a lot of work, but it's — yeah, it's pretty interesting."

When it was time to leave he waited until every other boy in the room had stood up; then he rose and turned so quickly, in such a flustered way, that she couldn't help noticing what he had to hide: there was a big wobbling bulge in the front of his trousers.

And she was embarrassed but shyly pleased. To think she could make a boy get that way just by sitting there — not moving around, not doing anything sexy at all — was enough to give her the self-confidence she'd lacked all day.

In the refectory, everything turned out to be fine. Larry Gaines did come and sit with her; he talked to her all through the meal in an intimate, husky murmur that was probably born of his having kissed her last week, and in walking her back through the quadrangle he asked her, shyly, if she would be his "date" at the Spring Dance.

"I'd love to, Larry," she said.

William Grove was reasonably sure she hadn't seen anything. He had stood up and turned away fast; the pants of his suit were amply pleated; besides, nice girls didn't look for things like that. Even so, it troubled him for days; it was still on his mind when Bucky Ward came into the office to ask him if he planned to go to the dance as a "stag."

"Oh, no," he said. "I'm not — I can't — what I mean is, I don't have a tuxedo."

"Couldn't your mother send it up?"

"No, I mean I don't *have* one."

"Oh. Well, look — " And Ward explained that his older brother, now in the Army, was about Grove's size; it wouldn't take more than a couple of days to have the brother's old tuxedo sent up to school by mail, and it would probably fit. Would that be okay? "Because the thing is," he concluded, "I'd really like you to meet Polly, Bill. I'd like her to meet you, too."

The tuxedo came just in time. It didn't fit, but the trouble was mainly in the over-large neckband of the dress shirt, and Ward convinced Grove that an ordinary white shirt would work just as well; nobody would notice.

Then the girls arrived. They arrived all through the afternoon, meeting their "dates" outside the One building archway and walking through the quadrangle under everyone's eyes. If they were made nervous by the scrutiny, by the clusters of walking or milling boys who stopped to stare, mouths partly open and partly smiling, they gave no sign of it. They looked and moved as if nothing in Dorset Academy could ever make them nervous, and they all had remarkably clean hair.

A slender, graceful, pretty girl paced the flagstones with Pierre Van Loon; before they reached Three building she hugged his arm and gave a thrilling laugh at something he'd said, while he trod along beside her with his toes pointed out as always, carrying her small suitcase. The watchers could only guess that Van Loon, however inconsequential he might be among boys, must be attractive to girls.

Art Jennings had a tiny girl, which was odd because he was so big. And she looked like the kind of tiny girl who knew how to have a good time, which was odd too because he was so shy.

Then came Steve MacKenzie with a girl everybody had to

agree was stacked. Even in her tailored spring suit you could
see the proud fullness of her breasts and hips — and the
funny part was that MacKenzie had lost all his customary
aplomb: he looked miserably bashful at having to parade her
past the observers.

Another great surprise was that Henry Weaver had a girl
— a real girl, not as pretty as some but perfectly all right-
looking, a girl who clung to his arm and whose skirt switched
nicely around her perfectly adequate, perfectly girl-like legs,
just as though everybody didn't know that Henry Weaver
was a queer.

When Grove saw Bucky Ward emerge from the One building archway with Polly Clark, he was careful not to stare.
Her face was in shadow anyway at first, so he wasn't missing
much; when he did look he found she was trim and nice,
neither beautiful enough nor fragile enough to warrant the
rapt, almost religious gravity with which Ward steered her
along.

All the rugs and a great deal of furniture had been removed
from the Knoedlers' big living room, which made it enormous. There seemed to be a hundred girls, spectacular in
their evening dresses, but there were probably more like
twenty. A small orchestra had been hired for the evening;
they played simple arrangements of popular songs, so
smoothly and with such an emphasis on the rhythm section
that even Grove felt he might be able to dance. But he remained paralyzed in the "stag line," along one wall, until
Bucky Ward danced up close and beckoned to him over Polly
Clark's shoulder.

"Oh," she said, holding up her sweet bare arms for him as

Ward moved away. "You're Bill Grove. I've heard *so* much about you."

"Well, I've certainly heard a lot about you, too."

She was exactly the right size for him. With his hand in the small of her back and her clean, fragrant hair just under his cheek, he felt manly and strong. He wouldn't have admitted it to anyone for the world, but this was the first time he had ever held a girl in his arms. Turning, he discovered what couldn't have been seen from where he'd stood against the wall. Two or three of the black windows on that side of the room were mottled with craning, grinning faces — boys who were either too young or too shy to attend the dance. They might well be laughing at him ("Hey, looka Grove! Looka Grove!") but he abruptly decided he didn't care.

"I'm afraid I don't dance very well," he said to Polly Clark, but she only tipped back her nice, smiling face and told him he was doing fine. That encouraged him to draw her closer, which she didn't seem to mind at all.

"I think it's so nice that Bucky has a good friend," she was saying. "He hasn't ever really had very many friends. He was sick a lot when he was growing up, you know, and he — "

"Yeah, I know."

" — and he never really had a normal — you know — a normal childhood or anything."

"Yeah."

He had always wondered, watching dancing couples, what the man could possibly do to hide the inevitable erection; now he was discovering that you didn't necessarily have to do anything: you could let it fill up against the girl until she would have to be a fool not to notice it; then when it stood upright you could use it as a brave and tender prod to suggest her every movement around the floor.

"You mustn't apologize, Bill," she said.

"Huh?"

"I said you mustn't apologize for your dancing; you're doing beautifully."

When Ward came back, tapping Grove's shoulder, Grove smiled at her and said "See you later, Polly," and walked away. The jacket of Ward's brother's tuxedo was double-breasted; no one could see the tumescence he brought back to the stag line; and suddenly it seemed very important to dance with as many girls as possible. The girl he wanted most was Edith Stone, but she looked so pleased with Larry Gaines that he wouldn't have dared; besides, common sense made clear that he couldn't "cut in" on a sixth former. That left almost half the girls, and he made the most of his opportunity.

"Oh, you're Pierre's roommate," Van Loon's girl said as Grove pressed her close. "It's very nice to meet you."

Then he tried Jennings' tiny girl and two or three others; he felt like a proud, bold lover, a smooth conqueror of many girls in that dizzy room.

When the orchestra struck up a waltz he retired to the wall to wait it out — he knew he could never perform anything as intricate as that — and from the wall he found it unsettling to watch Henry Weaver and his girl sweep past like professional ballroom dancers. Weaver's big, soccer-playing legs were able to do every subtle thing the waltz required, and more; his nice-looking girl seemed wholly at ease as she whirled and floated at his will.

But soon the music was simpler and slower, so he cut in on Bucky Ward again and took Polly Clark away.

"Hel*lo*, Bill," she murmured as he settled his cheek against her damp temple. And he danced with her three or four more times, until the band's slow opening strains of

"Goodnight, Sweetheart" announced that this would be the last number. After the first few bars of the song somebody turned the lights off, and they were moving and swaying in darkness. Grove knew there must be a good deal of kissing and feeling-up around the big room; he wanted to bend Polly Clark's head back and kiss her on the mouth, but lacked the nerve. Instead he held her tight and they moved only a little to the music, turning in place, and she seemed to be giving him as much of herself as the bondage of their clothing would allow. Over her shoulder he saw the dim tense shape of Bucky Ward on the sidelines, peering into the dark crowd, looking for her. He considered giving her up, but decided against it almost at once and took her deep into the middle of the room, where they stood clasped and swaying. Shyly, but with a thrust of unmistakable pride, she canted her hips forward. He knew there was supposed to be a sweet hard mound at the top of a girl's pussy, where the hair began, but he'd never truly expected to have it pressed and rubbing up against him to the moan of a saxophone. It was almost too much.

> *Dreams enfold you;*
> *In each one I'll hold you;*
> *Goodnight, sweetheart, goodnight.*

Less than a week later Grove found a small blue envelope behind the glass of his post-office box.

Ward, standing beside him, said "Well, I see you got a letter," and then drifted away to let Grove read it in privacy.

". . . I want to tell you again," Polly Clark had written in a neat, girlish hand, "how nice it was to meet you. Philadelphia isn't really very far from New York, so perhaps it might

be possible for us to meet again sometime. . . ." There was
an inconsequential paragraph, and then:

"I am fond of Bucky, but he doesn't *own* me. I hope you
will understand what I'm trying to . . ."

Grove finished the letter quickly and stuffed it into his
pocket, beginning to feel like a devil of a fellow. He avoided
Ward for the rest of the day, until Ward cornered him late
that afternoon in the Senior Club.

"So what'd she say?" he asked.

"Huh?" Grove felt his face getting warm.

"Oh, come on. I'd know that handwriting anywhere.
What'd she say?"

"Nothing much. Just said it was nice to meet me, and stuff
like that."

"You gonna write back?"

"Well, I — sure, I guess so."

Ward looked as if he were enduring physical pain. "It's
entirely up to you," he said. "Whether you write back or not
is entirely up to you." Then he turned and walked away past
the pool table, carrying his shoulders high.

"No, listen, hey, Bucky," Grove said, starting after him.
"Listen — wait a minute."

"Want to talk about it?" Ward said, not looking at him.
"Want to go outside?"

The bench behind the club was vacant, so they sat there
in silence for a long time, smoking, while the delicate moral
question hung in the air. Grove knew he would probably give
in — there seemed no other way to conclude this business
— but he wanted to let the tension last a while. He wanted
to savor his power over Ward as the minutes of silence went
by; and Ward seemed to be enjoying himself too, in a
wretched way.

In the end it was Grove's impatience with Ward's appar-

ent pleasure that made him say "Look: I won't write to her
if you don't want me to."

"It can't *be* because I don't want you to—don't you see
that?"

"Well then, it's because I don't want to," Grove said.
"Okay?"

"Okay," Ward said. "Okay, thanks." He looked as though
he regretted saying "thanks," but it was too late.

And not until an hour later, walking alone and thinking
of Polly Clark, did Grove begin to feel a sense of loss.

Another difficulty arose between them the very next week.
It was the time of double-room assignments again, and Grove
had scored a quiet triumph: Hugh Britt had agreed, with
almost no discussion at all, to be his roommate in the coming
year.

It had occurred to him that Ward might be a little hurt,
or jealous, but he wasn't ready for the look on Ward's face
when they happened to meet outside Three building. It
turned out to be even worse than the crisis over Polly's
letter.

"Let's take a walk," Ward mumbled, and they walked a
great distance — out past the infirmary and into the woods
and down a long hill, until they came to a small wooden
bridge across a glittering stream.

It was a lovely spot — the kind of place where lovers might
meet to discuss the impossibility of their situation, only to
fall into each other's arms in the end. And that was the
trouble: it *was* a place for lovers, not for anything as puerile
as the sad, silent display of Bucky Ward's hurt feelings.

"Here's the thing, Bill," Ward said after a very long time.

"When I saw your name and Britt's on the double-room list I felt — well, I felt let down, that's all."

"Yeah, well, I'm sorry you felt that way."

"The point is, I thought you and I were — you know, the best of friends — and I'd more or less assumed we'd be rooming together. That's all."

Grove didn't know what to say. He wanted to assure Ward that they were still "the best of friends," but he would be damned if he'd let Ward change his mind about rooming with Britt. He thought of Polly Clark's line — "he doesn't *own* me" — and felt as if Ward were trying to own him too. Above all, he resented having been brought to such a romantic place for such an embarrassing conversation.

And that made it all the worse when Larry Gaines and Edith Stone emerged through the trees, holding hands, walking slowly on their way back to school. Here was a real romance, with real lovers, and it made a mockery of whatever the hell else was taking place.

There were shy greetings — "Hi"; "Hi" — then Larry Gaines and Edith Stone walked over the little bridge and continued up toward the campus.

Edith had hoped it might happen that afternoon, in the clearing she had taken him to beyond the bridge, but all they'd done there, for the most part, was sit and talk. This was the third or fourth time she had hoped it might happen, and it hadn't. Larry liked to talk a lot, in a low, intimate voice, and he liked to kiss, often cupping one of her breasts in his hand while kissing; sometimes too he would run one hand down her back and let the other feel its way up the inside of her thigh, but he always stopped short; he always broke away from her with a heavy sigh and said something like "Oh, God, I love you, Edith."

And she was quick to answer that she loved him too, that she loved him terribly, but it was as if those declarations were all he needed. She knew there ought to be more; there would absolutely have to be more, in the very few days that remained before he went to sea.

Then suddenly it was his last night at school. Tomorrow he would go to New York wearing the seaman's clothes he had chosen for himself, the costume he was self-consciously modeling now in the Stones' house for Edith and her parents, for the Robert Driscolls and for a roomful of admiring boys: a new Levi jacket and pants, a knitted navy-blue "watch cap" worn low over one eyebrow, and rubber-soled work shoes.

"You look like you're on the high seas already, Larry," Robert Driscoll said. "You look as though nothing less than a German submarine could ever bother you."

Soon the other boys went back to the dormitories, the Driscolls went home, and it was time for Dr. and Mrs. Stone to go upstairs.

"Well, Larry, we certainly wish you luck," Dr. Stone said, shaking hands with him, "and we're going to miss you."

"Thank you, sir."

And Larry and Edith were alone. They began at once to clasp and writhe together, until Edith said "Oh, isn't there somewhere we can go?"

Larry Gaines thought it over. "Okay," he said at last. "We can go to the Senior Club."

But all the way out across the quadrangle, with his arm around her, he had to fight a rising sense of panic. He was a virgin. His plan, all along, had been to lose it with some nameless girl in Algiers, or wherever the Merchant Marine might take him — he had even thought he might contrive to develop a wide range of sexual techniques before coming home to Edith — but that excellent idea was closed to him now because she was crowding him; she wanted it; she wouldn't settle for anything less.

For more than a year he had kept an illustrated "marriage manual" among folded sheets in the linen bin beneath his bed, but he hadn't been able to learn much from it because whenever he read those lubricious paragraphs, in combination with those pictures, he would find himself helplessly masturbating. And he'd feel so rotten afterwards — was the President of the Student Council really supposed to jerk off? — that he would hide the book away again and swear off it entirely until the next time.

Now, for courage — or for luck — he said "I love you, Edith," as they walked under the dark trees, and she replied, as always, that she loved him too.

The Senior Club was filled with moonlight and shadows. The blue-gray scent of many cigarettes hung in the air, and around the leather sofa at the fireplace there was a faint lingering tang of woodsmoke from all the log fires of the winter and spring.

Edith stepped out of her shoes — that in itself was a pretty thing to watch — and put both hands behind her back to unfasten the hooks of her dress, letting a heavy lock of hair fall over half her face as she worked.

He fought his way free of the seaman's clothes, remembering only at the last moment to snatch the damned "watch cap" from his head; then he and Edith were naked and embracing and moving to the sofa, where he helped her to lie back on the wide, slick cushions, and he began to know from the very feel of her flesh in his hands that it was going to be all right.

At his first real thrust she gave a little whimpering cry that could have been pain or pleasure, or both, or neither, and he almost stopped to say "Are you okay?" but didn't because it seemed much better to keep going, to build and sustain a rhythm that would bring her along with him — oh, yes; now she was getting it — and soon nothing mattered at all but the strength and purity of their coupling.

It could have been midnight or noon. The Senior Club and the whole of Dorset Academy could have evaporated into the trees and even the trees could have vanished, for all they knew; they had overcome time and space in their need to help each other arrive at the heart of the world.

In the long aftermath they lay whispering together, saying things nobody else would ever be privileged to hear, and very gradually their circumstances closed in around them again: a smoking club, a preparatory school, a train that would have to be caught at eight o'clock in the morning.

". . . Can't find my cap," he muttered when he was dressed, groping along the shadowed floor.

"Oh, you've got to find the cap, Larry; it's adorable."

"Whaddya mean, 'adorable'?"

"You think that's something only silly girls ever say? Well, I don't mind; from now on I'm going to be the silliest girl in the world and you're going to love me anyway. . . . Hey, Larry?"

"Yeah?"

"Here it is. Your whaddyacallit. Your watch cap. It was in the fireplace."

"What the hell was it doing in the fireplace?"

"I don't know. But if you're really glad I found it, you know what you could do? You could come over here and hold me again for a minute. Just for a minute."

There were ten or fifteen minutes more at the moonlit door of her house, where they stood promising to write and to wait, saying again and again what each thought the other might most want to hear. "Okay, baby," he kept murmuring against her lips or in her hair, before he left her. "Okay, baby; okay."

Walking back to his room, he realized he had never called a girl "baby" before, and that alone — not to mention the astonishing impact of everything else — made him feel remarkably like a man.

There was little or no training. Less than two weeks after he left school, Larry Gaines signed on and shipped out as one of the thirty-man crew aboard a tanker bound for North Africa and riding low in the sea with its weight of military gasoline.

Ten miles out of New York Harbor, at about two in the morning, for reasons never investigated or explained, the tanker accidentally caught fire and exploded. There were no survivors.

It took several days for the news to reach Dorset Academy, and then it didn't break all at once. It crept and darted around the quadrangle from one cluster of stunned, unbelieving listeners to another; it seeped into faculty houses and into the kitchens of faculty wives; it went in and out of the infirmary and down to the baseball diamond and over to the track and back up to the Senior Club. More than a few people felt their faces twitch into foolish little smiles of incredulity on hearing it — smiles quickly covered with their hands. "I can't — it doesn't seem — I can't *believe* it," they said again and again. "Larry *Gaines?*" And by three or four that afternoon, everyone knew.

". . . He must've been asleep when it happened," Robert Driscoll said, hunched on his bed with his head in his hands while his wife massaged his neck and shoulders. "The whole crew must've been asleep at that time of night, except for whoever dropped the fucking cigarette, or fucked around with the fucking fuse box, or whatever the fuck it is you have to do to make a whole fucking ship blow up, and oh Jesus Christ Almighty, Marge. Oh Jesus. Oh Jesus fucking Christ Almighty."

"I know, dear," she said. "I know."

Myra Stone sat alone in her living room, twisting a moist handkerchief tight in her lap and feeling abandoned by everyone she had ever loved. Was this how things turned out in life? That you weren't even allowed to comfort your child in her grief because your husband said you were "too upset yourself"? Would everything always be this way? Would there never be an end to the pain of this rejection and this terrible, terrible loneliness?

Edith had been put to bed upstairs with what the doctor called a heavy sedative, but it wasn't working. Every fifteen or twenty minutes she would struggle upright, rubbing the heels of her hands into her face as if to rid herself of sleep, and say "Oh! . . . Oh! . . . Oh! . . . Oh!" Her eyes and mouth, in those moments, looked as though she might be losing her mind.

And her father would take her in his arms and help her to lie back on the pillow until she was still. "You have your whole life, Edith," he would say, each time. "You have your whole life."

Up in the *Chronicle* office the air was thick with smoke and dedication. Mr. Gold had agreed to break open the front page of the Commencement Issue for a two-column, three-inch, heavily black-bordered box, and he'd agreed to hand-set the type himself, but he had to have the copy by five o'clock and there were only twenty minutes left. Grove had

written four drafts, but Britt had found something wrong
with all of them ("Grove, you *can't* use 'As we go to press'
about a thing like this; don't you see that?"). For an hour
they had bickered and quarrelled and thrown crumpled
paper on the floor. Then Britt had loftily agreed to try his
own version and frowned over his pencil in enviable concentration, using his free hand to shield his work from Grove's
eyes. "No," he said at last, and began tearing it up.

"Hey, come *on*, Britt. Can't I even *read* the fucking
thing?"

"What's the point? It isn't any good; it isn't any better
than any of yours. Besides, it's not my job to do this. You're
the editor; *you* do it."

"Shit," Grove said. "Shit."

He was close to tears of frustration and fatigue, but the
high calling of letters brooked no compromise. He sat down
with a clean sheet of paper and the only pencil on the desk
that wasn't broken or dull. He knew Britt would be crouched
at his shoulder, watching every word, so he wrote the words
with an exaggerated care for their legibility.

It is a dark Commencement for the class of 1943.
Lawrence Mason Gaines, the outstanding member of
that class and one of the finest young men Dorset
Academy has ever known, died in the service of his
country last week. He was eighteen years old.

"That's it," Britt said quietly, "that's it; now the second
paragraph. You're getting it, Bill. You're getting it."

Chapter

In the following fall the class of 1944 were suddenly sixth formers — seniors — and most of them didn't feel up to it. Seniors had always been manly and dignified, fit companions for someone like Larry Gaines, and those standards seemed impossible to meet.

A few did well. Hugh Britt had been elected to the Student Council and was a model school leader, though some found him a little aloof. Jim Pomeroy and Steve MacKenzie were on the Council too, as was Gus Gerhardt. Anyone with the bulk, the athletic prowess and the blunt good looks of Gus Gerhardt would always be a natural for the Council, even if, as in Gerhardt's case, he was a slow and sullen bully.

The Presidency of the Council was an unconventional choice that year: it went to a short, tousle-haired boy named Dave Hutchins who was only moderately gifted at sports or studies, who looked younger than his age and didn't seem altogether sure of himself. His distinction was that everybody liked him, and he had drawn an unusually heavy vote from the lower forms.

"I know you're busy," Dave Hutchins said as he followed Grove upstairs to the *Chronicle* office one October afternoon, "but the thing is I was wondering if you might have time to help me with this speech I have to make. I think I've got it pretty well organized, but it needs a little — you know — a little help."

"Sure," Grove said, more flattered than he would have been willing to admit. "Let's take a look at it."

In the office they found Lothar Brundels sitting alone, looking up from the strewn pages of his humor column. Hutchins and Brundels had been close friends since they were both fourteen, in the third form, and they'd roomed together last year; but this year, in keeping with his position as top boy of the school, Hutchins had chosen to room with Gus Gerhardt. Grove watched closely for signs of awkwardness in their greeting but found none, and he guessed this was because nobody as nice as Brundels could hold a grudge against anybody as nice as Hutchins.

That was one of the funny things Grove had begun to learn about the senior class: the guys were *nice* to each other. There wasn't even any open scorn for Henry Weaver, or for the one or two other class pariahs, though of course those people were expected to be nice enough themselves to keep their distance.

"What's this speech of yours, Dave?" Brundels asked.

"Ah, Knoedler wants me to do it. It's about all the —

you know — the financial trouble we're in. The *school's* in,
I mean. He'll be making the main speech, when the parents
come for Thanksgiving, and he wants me to make a little
one. Nothing big. He gave me the general theme — 'If We
Fail' — and he must've talked for half an hour about the rest
of it, but I swear I didn't understand a God damn thing he
said."

Grove was going over Hutchins' three-page manuscript.
"Know what you might do, Dave?" he said. "You might work
in that Shakespeare business."

"What Shakespeare business?"

"You know, from whaddyacallit, from *Macbeth:* 'And if we
fail?' 'We fail. But screw your courage to the sticking place,
and we'll not fail.' "

"Nah, I don't know," Hutchins said, "I don't like that. I
don't like 'Screw your courage.' "

"Besides, it's all wrong, Grove," Lothar Brundels said.
"The people in the play are plotting a murder, for Christ's
sake. Don't you see the difference?"

In the end they got Hutchins' speech into reasonably good
shape — the parents, at Thanksgiving, would be made to
understand that their increased financial support was ur-
gently needed — then, after Hutchins had left, Grove turned
to Brundels and said "So what's the deal on all this, anyway?
Is the school gonna fold up, or what?"

"Shit, who knows? I know my father's looking for another
job."

"He is?"

"Been looking since last spring. And it hasn't been easy.
I mean northern Connecticut isn't exactly the best place in
the world for a chef to find work. And I heard Knoedler asked
the whole faculty to take salary cuts, and they told him to
shove it. They're all looking for new jobs too."

"They are?"

"Dr. Stone told me there've been faculty meetings where
they shout and argue and carry on like maniacs — that's the
way he put it — and he said they're all in a state of panic."

"He did?"

"Ah, you're a funny guy, Grove," Lothar Brundels said,
turning back to his humor column. "I mean you write pretty
well and you always get the paper out, but a lot of the time
you don't even know what the hell's going on."

Richard Edward Thomas Lear joined the Royal Canadian
Air Force in November. There was great applause in assembly on his last day at school, while he stood alone and pressed
his moist lips into a frown suggesting the spirit of the volun-
teer.

Several weeks later a similar ovation went up for Pete
Giroux, who was said to be failing most of his courses and
who now planned an immediate enlistment in the United
States Marines.

And those departures were only the beginning. The fed-
eral law that year required every male citizen to register for
the draft on his eighteenth birthday. There was a stipulation
for high-school seniors: if your birthday came before January you could be drafted during that month; if it came later,
the government would let you stay in school until the normal time of graduation in June. The three Dorset seniors
who fell into the first category had taken summer-school
courses to prepare them for a winter graduation; they received their diplomas in a makeshift ceremony one Friday
afternoon.

One of the three was Bucky Ward, and in honor of the
occasion Grove stayed up late with him in the *Chronicle*
office. They self-consciously passed a smuggled pint of whis-

key back and forth (it tasted so awful that Grove couldn't imagine the source of its celebrated power to give pleasure, let alone to enslave the soul), but they didn't have a very good time. Ward had recently gotten what he insisted on calling a Dear John letter from Polly Clark — she was engaged to an Army Air Force cadet — and he'd been dramatically morose for days.

"I don't care anymore," he announced, more than once. "I don't care what happens to me in the Army or anything else. If they make an invasion of France, I won't care if I'm the first little son-of-a-bitching rifleman on the beach. I mean that."

"Oh, balls."

"Whaddya mean, 'balls'? I'm only telling you how I feel."

"Yeah, yeah, okay; but shit, Bucky, everybody wants to live."

"Wanna bet? Listen: there are certain conditions of life under which I simply don't care whether my own life continues or not."

And the talk went on and on that way until the small hours of the morning, when Grove had begun to ache for sleep. At last he rubbed both fists in his eyes and said "Jesus, Bucky, you're going to be dead."

And Ward looked at him narrowly. "How exactly do you mean that?"

"You're going to be dead tired on the train tomorrow, going home. How the hell did you think I meant it?"

"I don't know. I'm not putting any more interpretations on anything anybody says."

With Ward gone, Grove was free at last to devote himself to Hugh Britt. Their being roommates had seemed to promise a great advantage, but soon there was trouble: a Germanrefugee boy named Westphal, who was Britt's chief rival for brilliance in the senior physics course, had begun to move in as Grove's chief rival for Britt's time.

Westphal spoke English with a katzenjammer accent that only Britt seemed able to understand, but he was clearly a "cultivated" boy, an "intellectual" beyond the reach of any plans Grove might have for himself.

All three of them were frightened of hockey, so they joined a large number of students who signed up for the alternate winter sport of "open skating." This meant that they skated in wide, easy circles around the outside of the embattled hockey rink on bitter-cold afternoons — or rather, Britt and Westphal did that, side by side in steady conversation, always at least thirty feet ahead of where Grove struggled on caved-in ankles, cursing his luck, hating the weakness of his own heart, while the Eagles and the Beavers beat each others' brains out on the ice within the shuddering boards.

There was one good thing: Bucky Ward had been the dorm inspector on the third floor of One building, where most of the seniors lived, and Grove was appointed to replace him. It didn't amount to much — seniors were too old and too nice to make any real trouble — but Grove loved the job.

"Get 'em *out!*" he would bellow down one corridor at Lights each night, and then, turning, "Get 'em *out!*" down the other. And he would check each room to see if anyone was missing. No one ever was. He would stand waiting at the stairwell for Driscoll's ritual visit — "Everything okay, sir" — and then he would saunter back to the room he shared with Hugh Britt, feeling pretty good.

Another good thing was that Westphal, however much of a fireball student he was and however nimble a skater, couldn't possibly have gotten the Dorset *Chronicle* out every two weeks. And even Britt had to admit that the paper was getting better all the time. The writing was livelier, the editing was more dependable, and the editorial that ran beneath the masthead in each issue often seemed, to Grove, to be a little triumph of prose composition.

"Well, but why do you spend so much *time* on the damn thing?" Britt demanded. "What're you killing yourself for? The whole school's going bankrupt anyway, everybody knows that. When the war's over, you think any college in America's going to care whether you put out the paper for some dopey little school that hasn't existed for years? Why don't you pay attention to your *grades*, Bill?"

Britt nearly always called Grove "Bill" now, and that in itself was bracing. Whenever he slipped back into calling him "Grove," Grove knew he'd probably said something dumb in the last day or two, and would sometimes lie awake trying to remember what it was.

Soon it was time for the seniors to take their College Board examinations; and because Dorset was less centrally located than Miss Blair's School, the authorities had arranged for the boys' exams to be given there.

This was a vaguely thrilling prospect. Apart from Gus Gerhardt, who was wholly familiar with the place but wasn't talking, nobody knew anything about Miss Blair's except that Edith Stone had graduated from it last year; but didn't it stand to reason there'd be other girls like her? They'd have long, clean hair and they'd stroll their campus in light flannel skirts and light cardigan sweaters, with their schoolbooks hugged close to their young breasts, and they'd say wonderfully engaging things like "Hi, my name's Susan."

Would the Dorset guys take their College Boards in a roomful of girls? And would they stay for lunch? And would there be time afterwards for strolling with the girls and getting acquainted, and maybe making "dates" for some weekend soon?

A long yellow bus stood waiting for them in front of One building, early one chilly morning. It didn't take long to reach Miss Blair's; they got there so soon, in fact, that most of the campus was still shrouded in morning mist. But the building where the bus let them off was plainly visible: it had a long second-story balcony at which eight or ten girls stood leaning out on their forearms, all wearing bathrobes, a few with their hair in curlers, and they were smiling and singing to their guests on the sidewalk below. It might have been fine, but then the words of their serenade came through, sung to the tune of "The Reluctant Dragon":

> *We are the Dor-set fairies*
> *Woo-woo; Woo-woo . . .*

The girls had composed only those two lines, so they sang them over and over like shrill, taunting children as the boys walked past beneath them toward the place on the ground floor where the College Board exams lay waiting.

It wasn't fair. Dorset Academy was a funny school — everybody knew that; but "Dorset *fairies*"? How could something like *that* have gotten into their minds? Grove squared his shoulders and walked with an exaggerated manliness to prove he couldn't possibly be a fairy, and he saw that Dave Hutchins, walking just ahead of him, was doing the same thing. He glanced quickly around to see how others were taking it, and he spotted Gus Gerhardt bringing up the rear of the wretched parade and blushing foolishly, just as one of the girls broke out of the song to call "Oh, not you, Gus; not you . . ."

There were no girls in the room where they took the College Boards, which lasted all morning and proved to be much more difficult than most of them had expected, and no plans had been made for them to stay at Miss Blair's for lunch. They climbed back into their bus — the upstairs balcony was empty now — and rode back to Dorset Academy with a sickening new awareness of what the term "funny school" might be taken to mean. Nobody wanted to talk about the girls and their song, and so it was never discussed.

There had been three or four air-raid drills a year in that part of Connecticut since the war began; by now they'd long become as much a matter of routine at Dorset as fire drills in a grammar school. But they were a nuisance: faculty families had to turn their living rooms into "shelters" for unwieldy numbers of boys, Robert Driscoll had to run around the campus like an air-raid warden, the whole Student Council had to report for duty taking roll calls in the shelters, then prowling to look for chinks of light.

And there was an air-raid drill in the spring of 1944 when everything went wrong for Dave Hutchins. The trouble started that afternoon when his roommate, Gus Gerhardt, saw him fitting a cone of heavy red plastic over the face of his flashlight.

"Whaddya doin' that for?" Gerhardt said.

"Air-raid drill tonight."

"Shit. Whadda they gonna do, send long-range bombers over from Berlin tonight? Or are they comin' from Tokyo?"

"Come on, Gus. It's just a thing we have to do."

"Who says?"

"Well, hell, *I* didn't make the rules."

"You didn't? I thought you made *all* the rules around here, Mr. President."

"Look," Hutchins said, and dropped the flashlight on his bed. "This thing of calling me 'Mr. President' is okay once in a while, when I know you're kidding, but it's getting to be a pain in the ass."

"Oh." Gerhardt turned his big head away to stare out the gray window. "Well. Sorry, Mr. President."

And he kept it up all through dinner. "Wait'll you see our President out there tonight," he said to several other boys at the senior table, well within Hutchins' hearing. "Think he'll let those long-range enemy bombers turn us into rubble? Wrong. He'll never let those long-range enemy bombers turn us into rubble."

By the time of the drill itself, Hutchins was badly shaken. He vowed he wouldn't risk seeming to pull his rank tonight, and to keep that promise he stayed well apart from the rest of the Student Council guys. He was standing alone in the darkness near Four building with his flashlight turned off, hiding from responsibility and waiting for the damned thing to be over, when Pop Driscoll came up to him and said "Dave? Is that you?"

"Yes, sir."

"How come those guys haven't turned their lights out over there?"

And Hutchins knew what he meant. Over in front of Two building, the whole width of the quadrangle away, the red-coned flashlights of the assembled Student Council glowed like burning cigarettes in the dark. Hutchins had stood here for ten minutes hearing the distant sound of Gerhardt's voice in the rhythm of a comedian's, setting up punch lines,

and at the expected intervals he'd heard all their laughter
rise and break and fall away.

"Hey, you guys!" Driscoll called. "Lights out over there!
Lights out!"

But they couldn't hear him across the quadrangle; it was
a windy night and the trees were making a lot of noise.

"Dave," he said, "run on over there and tell 'em to douse
those lights, okay?"

Hutchins would have given anything for the courage to
say *You* go; *you* go, Pop, but he went himself, jogging across
the dark flagstones. "Uh — " he began as he approached
them, and that brought on a happy chorus of "Uh — ";
"Uh — "

"Look," he said. "Mr. Driscoll wants you to turn off your
flashlights."

"Okay, Mr. President," several voices said.

He had turned away even before he heard that and started
to run back toward Four building, but he didn't make it; he
had to stop in the very center of the quadrangle, where he
could only hope the big trees would muffle small sounds, and
burst into tears against the heel of his hand.

It seemed very unlikely that any other President of the
Student Council had ever done anything like that.

For Driscoll, the most annoying thing about air-raid drills
was that they disrupted the normal process of getting the
kids bedded down; sometimes it was more than an hour after
Lights before all the dorms were quiet. But tonight his
rounds went fairly smoothly: it wasn't until he hit the second
floor of Three building that he found anything wrong.

The dorm inspector, a fourth former named Frank Bishop,
wasn't there to greet him on the landing, and when Driscoll

stepped inside to peer down both halls he felt a chill around his heart. One hall was dark and quiet, but the other — and this was Bobby's hall — was loud and bright with the light flooding out of a single room. It was Bobby's room, and as Driscoll hurried there, his shoes crunching a few spilled Ritz crackers on the floor, he wished he could remember some of the Catholic prayers of his childhood. "Oh, God help me," was all he could manage.

Bobby Driscoll, fat, naked and fifteen years old, lay splayed on his back across his bed. His face was hidden by a fully dressed boy who was sitting on it; four other fully dressed boys were pinning his limbs down, and one of them was rhythmically pumping his stiff, swollen prick in his hand. The boy doing the job looked up — it was Frank Bishop — and with a funny little twitch of mortified surprise in his face he said "Oh — hi, Pop."

"Everybody out," Driscoll said in the doorway. All the moisture had gone out of his mouth, but he could still speak. "Everybody out of here fast, and wait for me in your rooms. I'll be around to see you all shortly, and here's a piece of advice: you'd damn sure better be there."

Released from bondage, trying to hide his erection with his hands, Bobby skittered into bed, pulled the covers up and flopped over to face the wall. His straight, sweaty hair stuck out in all directions; nothing could be seen of his expression except that his temple and cheek were pink with shame.

Robert Driscoll closed the door, sat down on the edge of the bed and extended one hand to hold his son's shoulder. It seemed a long time since he had done that.

"Listen, Bobby," he said. "I want you to listen to me. This doesn't matter, do you understand me? This doesn't matter. It's just a dumb little thing that happens in prep schools. And the point is I don't want you worrying about it, Bobby.

I don't want you thinking there's something wrong with you, or anything like that, because there's nothing wrong with you, do you understand me? It was you this time and it'll be somebody else another time. It's just a dumb little prep school thing and it doesn't matter. Don't let it make you worry about yourself, will you promise me that? Do you understand me, son?"

Then he was out in the empty hall, the flashlight slippery with sweat in his hand. It was time to face the other boys in their rooms, one at a time, starting with Frank Bishop; and the trouble was that he didn't know what the hell he was going to say.

But he had made up his mind on one thing, anyway: as long as he lived, he would never tell Marge about this.

Mr. Gold broke out the largest typeface in the shop, never used before, in order to fill Grove's requirements for a front-page banner headline in the *Chronicle's* issue of April 20, 1944:

DORSET ACADEMY WILL CLOSE

Beneath that, down the top of the right-hand column, ran a three-line bank:

> Knoedler Cites
> 'Insurmountable'
> Fiscal Troubles

And then came the story, written exactly as Knoedler had asked for it, personally approved by him after three close readings, revealing nothing and enlightening no one in seven dense paragraphs with a runover on page two.

Grove's editorial in that issue spoke with what he'd hoped was eloquence of "our feelings" and "our emotions" on having "our worst fears confirmed." It wasn't one of his better editorials; he explained for days, to anyone who would listen, that it would have been better if he'd had more time.

With the news out at last, a sense of relief settled over the school. All anxiety and dread had come to an end in the luxury of collapse.

Marge Driscoll was vacuum-cleaning her rugs one morning, preparing them to be rolled up and stored for the summer, when it occurred to her to think: No, wait; we won't even *be* here this summer. Then she decided the rugs had better be rolled up anyway, for the moving van that would take all their stuff to wherever they'd be going; and it was another little shock to realize — as if for the first time — that she didn't know where they'd be going.

She switched off the vacuum cleaner and sat for a long time in a slowly settling cloud of house dust, thinking it over; she was still doing that when her husband came home and said "Honey, listen. Can you listen a minute? This is pretty important."

And he told her he'd just come from Knoedler's office. Knoedler had secured a job for himself as headmaster of a small new prep school in Michigan — it must have been something he'd worked on for months, during those protracted "drumming up trade" trips of his — and this morning, just now, he said he had learned there was a vacancy for an English master out there too.

"Oh?" Marge said.

"So first I tried to ask him about the school, and it turned out he doesn't really know much — I think he's so glad to have a job he doesn't care. All he could tell me was that it's — you know — that it's 'a good school.' Oh, and he told me they have interscholastic sports, because he knew I'd like that, which of course I do, and he said he couldn't quote the actual salary figure they'll be offering, but he said he was pretty sure it would be all right."

"I see," Marge said, carefully smoothing her skirt over her thighs. "Well, Bob, it's up to you. We'll talk it over some more — although of course it's too bad we don't have more information — and I think we ought to discuss it with Bobby too, don't you? He's old enough to have a part in making decisions like this. And then after we've all talked it over, you decide. Because you see in a thing like this, Bob, all Bobby and I can do is help you make your decision. Ultimately, it's up to you."

"Yeah," Driscoll said, looking tired. He took off his glasses, closed his eyes and pinched the bridge of his nose hard between thumb and forefinger. "Yeah, well, listen. Don't get mad, Marge, but here's the thing. I already said yes. I mean I already talked to the Michigan guy on the phone and I said yes to the whole fucking deal."

Three or four days later, on her way to the post office, Marge felt reasonably good. Things could be worse in this warm, wartime spring; it wasn't as if Bobby were of military age.

"Hi, Mom," one of the younger boys said, passing her in the quadrangle; it troubled her that she couldn't think of his name, but she put a little extra brightness into her answering "Hi" to make up for it. Then she saw Alice Draper up ahead and hurried to fall into step with her.

"How're you doing, Alice?"

"Oh, fair, I guess. Been doing a lot of typing; how about you?"

"Well, there's been quite a bit of typing in our house too," Marge said. That was a lie, but she'd promised Bob she wouldn't tell anyone about the Michigan job.

It was startling to see how shabby Alice Draper looked, as though she'd stopped taking care of herself months ago. Even now, Marge wasn't sure if she had ever "approved" of Alice's affair with La Prade — and she'd felt awfully sorry for Jack, as everyone had — but it couldn't be denied that Alice had *looked* better in those days; she'd been better company, too. Since then she had grown so drab, inside and out, that these little how're-you-doing talks were all Marge could muster for her. Even on their occasional shopping trips to Hartford, when Alice had once been all vivacity and urged Marge along with her until they'd giggled like schoolgirls all the way home — even those trips were dull and mostly silent now, and a relief to be done with.

"Oh, look, that's nice," Marge said in the post office. "You've got a letter from Jean-Paul."

"Ah, yes," Alice said in a flat voice. "That'll be pleasant for me, won't it. A little light in my life."

And Marge felt — well, irritated. Alice being cynical about Jean-Paul? Was there now nothing she *wasn't* cynical about? Could a person really be cynical about everything in the world and still expect to have friends?

"I'll see you, Alice," she said.

"See you, Marge." Then Alice Draper moved away toward home, walking very slowly in order to read the badly typed, single-spaced, three-page letter.

". . . And so I remain at my desk in Washington, wearing captain's bars but performing duties more appropriate to a corporal. My colleagues are mostly enlisted men, former graduate students and such, who openly resent my rank and pay. Yet every time I ask our commanding officer about an overseas assignment I am answered condescendingly in a language neither English nor French but pure U.S. Bureaucratic: no openings are contemplated in the foreseeable future. And oh, Alice, are you aware of what a deadly place this Capital City of yours is? Everything here is Spam and powdered milk and slow, hideously overcrowded taxicabs. . . .

". . . Alice, I hesitate to bring this up — it may only drive us farther apart — but there has been a chilling tone of indifference in your last few letters that I can neither account for nor understand. When you say, for example, that you are 'tired of feeling sorry' for me, I can only interpret that as meaning you find my unhappiness boring. Can this really be the voice of the woman I knew? If so, where did it all go, the passion and the love that nourished us both for so long?

"I knew from the start, of course, when we first met, that you found me 'romantic' only because your own life had grown dull; and so at any point in our time together I might easily have said I was 'tired of feeling sorry' for *you*. Do you see the irony here? Do you see the unfairness?

"Love is nothing unless it includes friendship — and how can we be friends, Alice, if I must sense in your letters the dwindling and cooling of your interest in me?

"Let me put it this way: Unless I soon receive a letter conveying some of the old vitality, the old spark, some suggestion of the Alice I knew, I will have no choice but to sever our correspondence. I hope . . ."

Alice finished reading just in time to pause at a big rusty trash container, out in the sandy area behind Four building. She tore the letter into halves, into quarters and into eighths; then she threw it away and went home.

Several hours later she was typing steadily, well into the
rhythm of it, making almost no mistakes and beginning to
feel a sense of accomplishment — did professional typists
feel this, after their first few days on the job? — but something had begun to bother her about the material she was
typing.

Jack Draper had come home a while ago from his final
class of the day. He was in the kitchen, finishing his second
drink, when he heard her machine clatter to a stop. For days
now — more days than he wanted to count — Alice had
worked and worked on this borrowed typewriter in the living
room, making many copies of his letter of application and his
employment résumé. When you wrote down the names and
addresses of all the private secondary schools in America
— and who cared which of them were "good" schools or
"bad" schools or any of the different kinds of "funny" schools
in between? — you ended up with quite a long list of places
to apply to for survival, and that meant a great deal of
typing. Today, he discovered on going into the living room,
she had worn an old pair of slacks for her work, and a badly
frayed shirt that had once belonged to him, and she'd put her
hair up, for business, under a hastily tied rayon bandana
that wasn't quite clean.

"Jack?" she said over her shoulder, looking briefly and
only partially away from the typewriter as he came in. "You
know this last paragraph of the résumé, where you explain
about your handicap? Well, look, of course I understand why
you put that in, but don't you think the résumé might be
stronger without it? Because of course most people aren't
going to care, but there could easily be someone who might,
and then you'd lose out on a job."

"Oh," he said, standing on the carpet ten feet behind her
chair. "You want me to misrepresent myself."

"I don't see it as misrepresentation at all. Under the circumstances, considering the spot we're in, I think it's only common sense." She was staring at the typewriter.

"Okay," he said, "fuck it. I don't care what the fuck you do with it. Do whatever the fuck you want."

And not even that dreadful little accumulation of "fucks" was enough to make her look up. She began typing again. He was determined that she'd look at him at least once before he left the house, and so, with one unsteady hand on the knob of the front door, he said "Alice?"

She turned around in a distracted way, her fingers tucking damp strands of hair up under the bandana. Her face, at that moment, looked weary and plain.

"Alice, I want you to know you're a lovely girl."

And he didn't even wait to see her expression — Bored? Puzzled? Pleased? — before he went outside and shut the door behind him. Not a bad line, he thought as his heels crunched the red pebbles of the walk to the science building. Later, when she thought about it, she might even come to understand that it was the best possible thing he could have said.

When he'd locked himself into the chemistry lab — no helpful young MacKenzie would find him this time — he stood for a while absorbing the silence and the shadowed emptiness of the place, with its pervasive smell of sulphur and the murmurous ghosts of its many, many classroom voices over the years. A faucet was dripping somewhere in the back; apart from that there were no sounds at all.

Twelve or fifteen matching chairs and small tables of lightweight blond wood were arranged to face the teacher's desk in a loose classroom formation, and he selected one chair-and-table set that had been shoved against the wall. He calculated the height of the chair, the height of the table,

and the height of an overhead steam pipe under the low
ceiling. These hazards could be overcome, even by a funny
little man who would have to stop and tremble and gasp for
breath at each stage of his climb. Kneel on the chair first, his
funny little body counselled him. Bring one foot up —
good — and now the other. Take your time. Now hold onto
the wall — steady — and stand. Good. Now the table. Kneel
first; one foot up; hold the wall; now the other foot; stand.
Wow.

It might have been dizzying to stand erect on a tabletop
and see the chemistry lab from this odd new perspective, but
nothing on earth could have made Jack Draper queasy now.
He felt triumphant.

One of the better things about Brooks Brothers was its line
of leather belts. Supple, sturdy, made in England, they were
more than adequate for holding up your pants. You could
pass the buckle end of one over a convenient steam pipe,
make a loop and pull it tight, then bring the other end
around your neck and tie it in a firm, excellent knot at the
side, just under one ear.

"Okay, Alice," Jack Draper said aloud into the empty
room. "Okay, baby. I love you."

But he couldn't kick the table away. Any normal man,
with normal legs, could easily have sent it crashing in less
than a second, so that he'd drop and catch and spin —
and the whole fucking world would end forever; but Jack
Draper stood trembling and helplessly alive, treading the
table in his pitiable shoes. He could work a toe back under
the rear edge of the table but didn't have the strength to
upset it that way; he could work a heel over the forward edge
but couldn't turn it over that way either.

"Come *on,*" he said, almost whimpering. "Come *on;* come
on."

And for what seemed half an hour, though it was probably more like ten minutes, he tried and tried. He would rest, sweating, breathing hard, gathering strength, and try again. No luck.

"Draper, Draper, you're an idiot," he said. "You're an asshole. You can't even do a simple fucking thing like this."

The knot of the belt had begun to creak faintly under his ear with each breath. The only way to stop the creaking was to untie it; when he'd done that, the belt looked so wretched dangling from the pipe that he took it down.

And getting down, for reasons he didn't even try to understand, was harder than getting up had been. Bracing himself against the wall as he lowered one badly shaking foot to the chair, he was terrified that he might crumple and fall. Wasn't this the God damnedest thing?

When he was safe on the floor at last, working the damned belt back through the waist-loops of his pants, he knew only that he was ready for a drink. And he wouldn't settle for the warm piss from the tank here in the lab, either: he would have bourbon, in a big glass with plenty of ice, and he would have it seated at the kitchen table of his own home, like a man.

There was barely time to fix the drink, and to settle down with it, before Alice came to stand in the kitchen doorway. She looked troubled and oddly shy.

"I decided you were right about that," she said.

"Right about what?"

"That place in the résumé, where you tell about your handicap. I was wrong, that's all, and I'm sorry."

"Oh. Okay."

"Because of course it's better your way. It's more honest

and it's more courageous. I was just — I don't know; I'm sorry, that's all." One of her pale, slender hands came up to clasp the other at her waist; the two hands writhed together there while she seemed to gather courage. "And Jack?" she said.

"Yeah?"

"That was nice, what you said."

"What'd I say?"

"That I was — that I'm — you know. A lovely girl." And she started to cry, but recovered quickly. If she cried, she explained, wiping her tears, she wouldn't be able to talk — and oh, there were so many things to say. Would he mind very much if she came over and sat with him?

This couldn't be real: good whiskey in his veins, with plenty more where it came from; Alice close and warm beside him for the first time in God only knew how long, pouring her heart out in an avalanche of tenderness. And all he had to do was sit here and let it happen; sit here and take it in. Wow.

". . . and Jack, remember when you first came out of the hospital, and you kept saying 'Baby, I'm a basket case'? And do you remember what I said?"

"No."

"Oh, I was hoping you'd remember, but if you don't I'll tell you. I said 'You're just the kind of basket case I've wanted all my life.' "

Well, all right, swell, he thought. That's nice; she's sorry; she wants to come back; we'll kiss and make up like people in the movies. But what are we ever going to do about the year and a half with Frenchy La Prade?

And while he was in this cool, discriminating mood it occurred to him that he might as well admit she wasn't really a very pretty girl. She probably never had been, except in his own lust-crazed vision, even in the best of the old days. There was too much nervous motion in her face, for one thing; besides, wouldn't it be better if her eyes were just a tiny bit farther apart? And besides, didn't everybody know that a girl of her age could hardly be called a girl anymore? Oh, a woman could be splendid too, of course — everybody knew that — but what about a woman who had opened her legs three and four times a week for a year and a half to welcome a muscular, posturing son of a bitch who probably looked, when naked, like an old-time photograph of the male model in the "life class" of some third-rate Paris art school at the turn of the fucking century?

Oh, yeah, yeah, there was the hell of it; there was the trouble. What would they ever be able to do, now, about Frenchy La Prade?

". . . and you're such a *brave* man, Jack," she was saying. "Oh, I know you hate that — you've always said handicapped people hate to be called 'brave' — but I don't mean it in that sense alone. The way you sort of — carry on; the really gallant way you face each day in this awful, awful little place — oh, and Jack, have you any idea how much the children love you?"

It was the word "children" that tore him apart and made him feel good at the same time. "Children" was the word that sent blood flowing heavily into his groin, filling his prick, so that the only thing in the world to do was scrape back his chair and struggle to rise.

Alice helped him, murmuring something sweet that he couldn't quite hear. She put her arm around his back; she took and held his funny little hand and matched her steps to those of his funny little feet, and they walked together, carefully, to their bed.

*   *   *

Abigail Church Hooper let it be known to Knoedler, through
her lawyers, that she wished to invite the senior class to her
home for tea some afternoon before the end of school.

"It'll be a chore, Bob," Knoedler said to Driscoll, "but
there's no one else I'd trust with it."

And so in a short parade of cars, with Driscoll driving the
first one, the class rode the ten miles of highway to old Mrs.
Hooper's estate. None of them had ever seen it before.

She had evidently bought or built her home before devel-
oping her passion for "Cotswold" architecture. The mansion
was Victorian and ugly — not even the elegant blue awnings
at all of its many windows could save it — but it certainly did
look like money.

A middle-aged manservant appeared on the freshly raked
pebble driveway to tell Driscoll where the cars were to be
parked; then Driscoll and the boys were inside the place,
walking down a long wide hall hung with brown oil paint-
ings, and suddenly there she was: a small, fat old woman in
purple, seated with her knees well apart and with her back
to the far wall of a big panelled room. A cane rested against
one arm of her chair.

". . . Driscoll?" she said, extending one liver-spotted hand,
palm down. "That's an Irish name. Are you from Boston?"

"No, ma'am. I come from New Jersey."

"Oh. Well, but then it always has been difficult to keep
track of the Irish, hasn't it? Is this really the whole of the
senior class?"

"It was a small class to begin with, Mrs. Hooper," he said,
"and several of the boys have left to join the service."

They were already forming a ragged line to one side of the
old lady's chair — they seemed to sense what was expected

of them here — and Driscoll introduced them one by one as they filed past and took her hand.

". . . Weaver?" she said. "That's a good English name. . . . Van Loon? Oh, that's a fine old Dutch name. . . ."

A maid came in, trundling a big tea cart — there would be tea and tiny squares of sponge cake to ease their discomfort in this house — and for twenty minutes or so the boys were left to themselves. They wandered around the room and back into the front hall to inspect the decorations. Then Driscoll tapped Dave Hutchins on the shoulder and said Mrs. Hooper was ready to talk to them all.

"Okay, sir," Hutchins said, and turning away he called "Hey, you guys — I mean, uh, you boys — "

And Driscoll got a chuckle out of that. Little Dave Hutchins, President of the Student Council and certainly the most agreeable kid in school, had been afraid that "you guys" might be just the note of strident vulgarity that could make this mansion crumble and fall.

They gathered around her then, most of them sitting on the carpet — nice kids, polite kids, kids whose fathers had spent far too much to send them through a funny little school that nobody ever heard of, who only last month had learned their school was bankrupt and who very likely did feel some of the "emotions" described in Grove's fervid editorial, but who for the most part, bless them, probably didn't give much of a shit.

"Gather around me, boys," Mrs. Hooper said, as though she'd rehearsed that line and was determined to deliver it even though they'd already gathered around her. "I'm very glad to see you all today because you're the last graduating class of what I shall always think of as — my school.

"I always wanted to be a boy, you know. Oh, yes — " And here her puckered lips came apart to reveal glistening, smiling false teeth — "oh, yes; as a child, as a girl, I always

wanted to be a boy. Because men *do* things in the world, you
see. Men *run* the world. And so, not long after my late husband's death, I had a dream. I dreamed of a school for boys
that might be just the kind of school I'd have wanted if *I'd*
been a boy. Do you see? Well, it's all gone now, isn't it?

"But I want you to know I tried to save it. I tried for years.
I don't wish to discuss your man Knoedler today because I
have my blood pressure to think about, but I'll tell you this
much: he never understood Dorset Academy. He never understood Dorset Academy at all. So now it's gone — all my
years of work and planning, all my devotion. All gone. And
I understand you boys are going into the Army and that sort
of thing.

"Well, my father was a cavalry officer with General Burn-
side in the Civil War. He was decorated three times, and oh,
my, he was a handsome figure. I'll never forget how fine he
looked on horseback, even in later life. He was a man born
to ride. And now of course there's no cavalry anymore, is
there, so you boys will miss all that. I expect you'll be push-
ing automatic buttons sort of thing in this dreary war of Mr.
Roosevelt's.

"I call it Mr. Roosevelt's war, you see, because I believe it's
only part of his plan to turn us all into Communists and
Negroes. Have you thought of that? You may ask how it's
possible to turn people into Negroes, and I'll tell you. The
male Negro has an enormous — an enormous procreative
power. That's his one great advantage over most white men,
you see, and then of course there will always be impression-
able white girls. So you have two or three generations of
Communist propaganda, you see, and there you are. Well,
Mr. Murphy? Mr. Murphy?"

"Yes, ma'am, I'm sorry; my name's Driscoll."

"Yes, well, unless some of the boys have questions, I'm
feeling a little tired."

There were no questions.

Going home, going back to school, Driscoll turned once from the wheel of the first car in their little motorcade and started to say something like "Guess you guys are glad to be out of *that* sweatbox, huh?" but he swallowed the impulse. It wouldn't have been tactful; it wouldn't have been what Knoedler called discreet. Besides, the boys did seem to have gotten through the afternoon with no great strain: they had chewed their sponge cake and sipped their tea and listened with apparent patience to the old woman's talk; it may not have been much worse than paying a dutiful visit to their grandmothers, if they had grandmothers — and some of them, come to think of it, probably came from families rich enough to have grandmothers every bit as awful as that.

There was one final announcement concerning Dorset Academy's bankruptcy. The United States Army, Knoedler said at assembly one day, had leased the buildings and grounds, the "physical plant" of the school, to use as a rehabilitation center for blinded veterans. The men and their medical staff would begin to occupy the premises immediately after graduation.

That was a nice break for Grove: it gave him the material he'd lacked for his editorial in the Commencement Issue. He worked on it for days; when the final draft was finished, just before the deadline, he offered it up for Britt's approval.

A SALUTE

It is fitting that Dorset Academy, on delivering its final senior class to the war, will now serve to accommodate blinded Army veterans.

Men who have lost their sight in combat can hardly be expected to take comfort in a greeting of any kind as they feel their way into a dark and bewildering new place; even so, the class of 1944 would like to offer them this assurance: There is nothing to fear here. We here before you have seen it all.

We have seen the play of sun and shadow on the blood-red stone and sweeping slate of these beloved buildings. We have seen the trees. We can watch one another rise today to take our diplomas; we can remember how each of us looked in saying goodbye.

Our vision will guide us through military training, but soon, as we move out to the battlefronts of the world, there will be no further certainties. We will then enter into our own time of blindness — if not in the physical, surely in the spiritual sense of the word. And when we come back, if we come back at all, it will be to find ourselves forever changed.

You, the young soldiers soon to occupy our dormitories, have far less reason for hope than we do, but our hope is qualified too; and so in a spirit of comradeship we salute you.

Welcome, veterans. Blind though you are, embittered though you may be, rest well here and learn what you can. This place is yours.

"That's nice, Bill," Britt said. "I think it's the best one you've done."

"Well, it sure as hell oughta be," Grove said. "It took me about forty-nine fucking hours."

"There's just one thing. In the third paragraph, I'd take out 'beloved' before 'buildings'. You don't really 'love' the buildings, do you?"

"I guess not."

"Okay," Britt said. "It'd be stronger without that word. But the rest of it's very nice."

In the Stones' house it was Edith who did the typing. She was good at it — she had worked all year as a secretary in the headmaster's office — and the sound of her steady, rapid drumming on the machine seemed a terrible reproach to her mother as she puttered aimlessly in the kitchen or tried to rest upstairs.

Didn't everyone need and deserve to feel useful sometime? Even if only near the end of a lonely, neglected life? Oh, they'll miss me when I'm gone, Myra Stone thought, but the worst part was that she couldn't even be sure of that.

Dr. Stone spent much of his time on the telephone. Application letters and résumés were all very well, but for a man of his age, with his credentials, a decent job was more likely to come about through personal contacts.

". . . Howard?" Edith heard him saying. "Edgar Stone here . . . Oh, we're all well, thanks, and how've *you* been? How's Ellen? . . . Good, good. Howard, there's been something of a disaster here; the school's gone bankrupt, and I wondered if you might know of any — what? . . . Oh, the usual sort of mess; years of mismanagement and so on; but I was wondering if you might know of any . . ."

Edith got out of the house before waiting to hear the end of that conversation — it was too much like all the others that had come to nothing — and set off to take her finished stack of mail over to the office, where she would place it in the "Out" basket. On her way there, in the quadrangle, she looked up to find she was walking beside a boy she had always rather liked and never paid much attention to —

Bill Grove. He was out of breath; apparently he'd been running to catch up with her.

"Hello there, Bill."

"Hi, Edith." There were people who said Edith Stone had looked "awful" since Larry Gaines' death, but she still looked pretty nice to Grove.

"That's a funny thing," she said. "I was just thinking about you."

"You were?"

"Because my father was talking about you last night. He thinks you're a good writer."

"He does?"

"Oh, come on; you knew that. People who're good at something never need to be told. Anyway, I wanted to wish you a lot of luck in the service. When do you think you'll be going in?"

"Oh, right after graduation, I guess."

"Well, look," she said, coming to a stop at the little path to the office, and she swept back her hair with one hand in order to look up at him. "I may not see you again before — you know; before school's out — so take care of yourself, okay, Bill?"

"Thanks — and you too. You too, Edith."

He hoped she might pause on the path and turn back to wave, or maybe even to blow him a kiss — that would be a marvelous thing to take into the Army — but she went on walking all the way to the door and inside, her hair floating at her sweet shoulders and her skirt shifting nicely around her legs.

Then it was the last day of school. Classes were only a formality and some of the masters barely managed to turn up

for them, but it was considered important to keep everyone
on campus because tomorrow was Commencement Day. Parents would be arriving from all over, most of them scarcely
able to hide their indignation. What parents, after all, would
ever have sent a son to this school if they'd had any idea it
was failing, that it would hit the skids and go down and out
like some sleazy little commercial venture?

And the Commencement ceremony itself, no matter how
hard everyone tried, would almost certainly be a lame and
awkward thing. Still, they would all have to go through with
it.

Robert Driscoll was uneasy all day about the possible
kinds of trouble there might be in the dormitories tonight,
but nothing prepared him for what he found on his rounds:
almost the whole of the sixth form, the graduating class, was
missing. Henry Weaver and two other social outcasts were
the only seniors in their rooms.

"Is this supposed to be some kind of a prank, or what?"
Driscoll asked, letting his flashlight stare into Weaver's
wincing, blinking face. "Where are they, Weaver?"

"I don't know, sir."

And Driscoll decided to drop the beam of the flashlight to
Weaver's chest. Even a pariah might have sensitive eyes.
Then Weaver said "You might try Ed Slovak's house. The
guy that works in the power plant? You know him? He's
friendly with a few of the guys; there was some kind of talk
about a party there."

"Oh. Okay, thanks."

And Driscoll did know Slovak, a big, smiling man in a dirty
T-shirt, always scratching his armpits, as if it had never
occurred to him that taking a bath and changing his shirt
might get rid of the itch. The Slovaks lived in a raw clap-
board bungalow strung with many electrical wires, on a

patch of bald earth just inside the woods a few miles down
the road.

Driscoll had started up his car before he realized that a car
wouldn't do the job; instead he went to the school garage and
got the big yellow pickup truck.

The Slovaks' house was ablaze with light when he brought
the truck bouncing to a stop in the turnaround of its dirt
driveway, and he could see the heads and shoulders of many
boys inside. But he was greeted at the door by a haggard,
Spanish-looking man of about his own age — one of the
kitchen help, still wearing the stained whites of his day's
work.

"Nobody here," the man said.

"Come on. I'm from the school." And Driscoll showed him
the extinguished flashlight in his hand, from the hip, as if it
were a badge.

They were all there, in the kitchen and small living room
of this crude house, with its bright mail-order furniture and
its blaring radio, and four or five other kitchen-help men
were among them. Mrs. Slovak, a plump woman in a floor-
length housecoat and dirty pink slippers, was too intent on
fussing with the radio dials to notice his arrival, but her
husband, standing near the liquor supply, was very much
the jovial host.

"Mr. Driscoll!" he called. "What's your pleasure, sir?"

"No, thanks," Driscoll called back. "Not tonight."

None of the boys looked really embarrassed at his en-
trance — and why should they? How could it really be said,
now, that they were doing anything wrong? With the exception of Van Loon, who was conversing with a befuddled-
looking kitchen man, they didn't even seem to have been
having a very good time. Some looked drunk — poor Dave
Hutchins looked ready to pass out, or throw up, or both

— but they all faced Driscoll with a suggestion of relief, as though they were glad rather than sorry that he'd come for them.

"All right, listen," he announced, raising his voice to compete with the radio. "I think it's about time we broke this up. I've got the truck outside."

Then he left the house and stood in the dirt near the open tailgate. He knew they'd come out without coaxing, and they did. "I'm surprised to see you here tonight, Dave," he said, "and you too, Hugh." But Hutchins was too tired or ill to answer, and Britt only gave him a look as melancholy as anything in the Russian novels he'd been reading.

"Get on in there," he said as they came singly or in clusters, swaying toward the truck. "Get on in there." Jennings, Pomeroy, MacKenzie, Westphal, Van Loon . . .

And finally, the last to leave the party, came Grove. For three years now, Driscoll had wondered what it was that put him off about this particular kid. Was it just that he couldn't run or throw or catch, and that he'd daydreamed his way through school and done badly everything but the courses he liked? Well, yes, and then there was his self-dramatizing role as *maestro* of the damned school paper (and why *had* Knoedler let him do that, with failing grades?). There would probably always be kids like Grove in prep schools: you would find only irritation in trying to help them, or to like them, and you could probably never bring yourself to call them by their first names until ten years later, when they came back to visit the school with their wives.

"Well, Mr. Dorm Inspector," he said. "I suppose you realize that under normal conditions you'd be in bad trouble tonight."

"Yes, sir."

"Why'd you do this, Grove? Huh? Why'd you want to pull a silly stunt like this?"

And Grove lowered his eyes. "I don't know," he said. "We just thought we'd — I don't know. I mean everything's over anyway, isn't it?"

"Yeah," Driscoll said. "Yeah, everything's over. Okay." Then, without quite realizing what he was up to, he clapped the boy hard on the shoulder in what anyone would have said was affection. "Okay, Bill. Get on in there."

And it hadn't really cost him anything to say "Bill." How could he have saved that for a better time when there would now be no other times at all?

When Grove had vaulted awkwardly into the truck, Driscoll slammed the tailgate shut and secured it with the heavy little hooks on the heavy little chains. Then he walked around to the driver's seat and started up the engine and set off for home, taking them back to school.

There were no lights along the road, and it was speckled with spine-jolting pot holes that wouldn't be repaired until after the war. Driving wasn't easy, if you weren't used to a truck, and Driscoll was grateful to let that occupy most of his mind, but then he heard them singing.

He had known they would probably sing, but he'd expected some war song, one of the bawdy, rollicking soldiers' songs with many verses that every kid in America must know by now, like *Roll Me Over,* or *Bless Them All.* Instead, in hesitant voices, they had taken up a tame little college boys' beer-drinking song that he remembered from his own freshman year at Tufts, long ago:

> *Drunk last night;*
> *Drunk the night before;*
> *Gonna get drunk tonight*
> *Like I've never been drunk before . . .*

There was no readiness for soldiering in this truck, no stern and cocky welcoming of challenges. They sounded — oh, Mother of God — they sounded like children.

> *Sing glo-o-rious,*
> *Glo-o-rious,*
> *One keg o' beer*
> *For the fo-o-ur of us . . .*

And Robert Driscoll was damned if he knew how anyone could blame him, ever, for what he did then. He slowed down to twenty-five miles an hour, for safety; he hunched over the wheel and held it tight in both hands; he kept one eye open and steady on the road, and he let everything else fall apart inside him while he cried and cried.

Afterword

Pierre Van Loon died of shrapnel wounds inflicted by German artillery in the last week of what came to be known as the Battle of the Bulge.

A month later, on the other side of the world, Terry Flynn was killed in the second or third assault wave on the beach at Iwo Jima.

Those, with Larry Gaines, are the only Second World War deaths I'm certain of among the boys I knew at Dorset Academy. There may well have been others, but without the Alumni News column it was impossible to know.

*   *   *

I saw Bucky Ward briefly in 1946 and '47, in New York, and he was full of war stories. He limped a lot, saying he'd been wounded in the knee and had refused a Purple Heart, but there were embarrassing times when he would walk the streets for miles, deep in conversation, without limping at all. He talked of having repeatedly volunteered to serve as first scout on dangerous patrols and of taking personal risks that caused other men to say "No! Don't!" Twice, he said, once in the Bulge and again at the Siegfried Line, the force of concussion from enemy artillery had "blown every stitch of clothes off my back — when the guys got to me I was lying there naked as a baby." And all this had sent him home with a profound new sense of his own potential value to mankind.

"It's only reasonable to wonder why I was saved," he explained, staring earnestly into his coffee in a Bickford's cafeteria at one o'clock in the morning. "Why me? Out of all those others, why me? Oh, I'll never be sure, I suppose, but I think I know. I think it's Christianity. I think it's Jesus." And so he had resolved to become a man of the cloth. I haven't seen or heard from him in thirty years.

I corresponded with Hugh Britt until about 1950, often writing two or three drafts of my letters to improve the prose. Though he hadn't talked much about it in our last months at school, Britt had been accepted into a Navy program called the V-12 that allowed bright students to enroll as Naval personnel in civilian universities, where they could rapidly earn both bachelors' degrees and Naval Reserve commissions. Britt attained those goals soon after the war, without ever having left the Middle Western city of his birth; he was also married by then, and a father. Next came medical school, for which he was amply prepared, and in one of his last letters he said he thought he would be a psychiatrist. I was the one who stopped writing letters: the strain of trying to keep up with him had worn me down at last.

One day in 1955 I ran into Steve MacKenzie walking along Lexington Avenue. We had a few beers and laughed more than we meant to and punched each other's arms; in the end, out on the sidewalk again, I think we shook hands about three times in saying goodbye. Just before turning away he said "Listen, though: don't look back too much, okay? You can drive yourself crazy that way."

My father has been often on my mind lately, perhaps because in four more years I will be as old as he was when he died. My mother is long dead too, now, and so is my sister — she died young — but it is my father who haunts me most.

I keep trying to picture him as a young man, before the General Electric Company got him, when he was traveling alone around upstate New York and determined to sing for a living. He must have been brave and tense and more than a little self-important then, yet often tired and ridden with terrible doubts, until he gave up.

All I'm really qualified to remember is the sadness of his later life — the bad marriage that cost him so much, the drab little office from which he assisted in managing the sales of light bulbs for so many years, the tidy West Side apartment, redolent of lamb stew, where I can only hope he found love before his death.

Still, even now, his singing is what I try to remember best, the splendid lyric tenor voice that rang from the walls of my early childhood. Once ten years ago, driving across the middle of America late at night with the car radio buzzing and crackling in the dashboard, I suddenly heard a high, pure ribbon of sound; and there he was, if only for a moment, a young concert tenor in some town a thousand miles away:

. . . But come you back
when summer's in the meadow,
Or when the valley's hushed
and white with snow . . .

Then he was torn away on the air and the static closed in,
and the commercials, and an all-night preacher in Missouri
wanting to tell me about salvation, until I turned the thing
off and tried to concentrate on the road.

If my father had lived I would certainly have thanked him
for paying my way through Dorset Academy. I know he
never trusted the place, and for that reason I would have
persisted if he shrugged-off my thanks. I might even have
told him — and this would have been only a slight exaggera-
tion — that in ways still important to me it *was* a good
school. It saw me through the worst of my adolescence, as
few other schools would have done, and it taught me the
rudiments of my trade. I learned to write by working on the
Dorset *Chronicle,* making terrible mistakes in print that
hardly anybody ever noticed. Couldn't that be called a lucky
apprenticeship? And is there no further good to be said of the
school, or of my time in it? Or of me?

I will probably always ask my father such questions in the
privacy of my heart, seeking his love as I failed and failed to
seek it when it mattered; but all that — as he used to suggest
on being pressed to sing "Danny Boy," taking a backward
step, making a little negative wave of the hand, smiling and
frowning at the same time — all that is in the past.